An outbreak of a rare, dangerous fever, with contacts somewhere up in the hills of the Drakensberg—this was how Sister Laura Kent found herself, together with Dr David Mackay at the hospital in the hills, working with him in a life-and-death struggle

Elizabeth Scott, who was born in Scotland and now lives in South Africa, is happily married, with four children all in their twenties.

She has always been interested in reading and writing about anything with a medical background. Her middle daughter is a nursing sister, in midwifery, and is her consultant not only on medical authenticity, but on how nurses feel and react. She wishes she met more doctors like the ones her mother writes about!

HOSPITAL IN THE HILLS

BY

ELISABETH SCOTT

MILLS & BOON LIMITED
15-16 BROOK'S MEWS
LONDON W1A 1DR

First published in Great Britain 1987 by Mills & Boon Limited

© Elisabeth Scott 1987

Australian copyright 1987 Philippine copyright 1987 This edition 1987

ISBN 0 263 75722 6

Set in Monotype Times 10.8 on 11 pt. 03–0487–51488

Typeset in Great Britain by Associated Publishing Services Printed and bound in Great Britain by Collins, Glasgow

CHAPTER ONE

Sister Laura Kent was never sure, afterwards, just when she began to be aware that something was wrong.

The huge hospital looking across Cape Town to Table Mountain was always full of doctors and nurses going about their duties swiftly and efficiently. Often you would see two doctors standing talking, grave, absorbed, serious. Often you would see a nurse walking swiftly along the long polished corridors, so intent on her job that she might not recognise one of her own set until she had passed. Often you would find that a patient had been transferred to another ward, with no warning.

So—there was nothing in any of these happenings to account for the feeling of strain, of tension, that Laura gradually became aware of. Nothing to account for the slow-growing certainty that something very serious was happening at the hospital.

Before she heard anyone begin to talk about it, before the rumours began, Laura felt all this. She felt it right away, she thought later, because this was her hospital. She had trained here, and she had become a Sister here, and there were few of the wards she hadn't worked in at some time during these years.

And so she knew that she wasn't imagining that something very far removed from the usual was disturbing the bustling efficiency of St Luke's.

After a day or two of becoming more and more aware of this, she mentioned it, tentatively, to her friend Jane. Laura and Jane, with Penny, who was currently on night duty, had started as student nurses together, and the bond forged then had never been broken, for all three were now Sisters—very new Sisters, they admitted, but Sisters—Laura on one of the Surgical wards, and Jane on Casualty, and Penny on Medical. There was that special closeness between the three of them that made it possible for Laura to ask Jane if she had noticed anything strange, different.

'I can't say I have, Laura,' Jane said, after a moment's consideration. She looked around the crowded hospital canteen. 'Everything looks fairly normal to me. The steak's as tough as ever, and the peas as overcooked!'

Laura, too, looked around, but after a moment she shook her head.

'No, not here, Jane. In the hospital itself. In the corridors, in the wards—I don't know, I can't explain it.' She smiled, with difficulty. 'I must be imagining things.'

'I wouldn't be too sure of that,' her friend replied. 'Remember, down in Casualty we're rather cut off from the rest of the hospital, we move from one crisis to the next, and things happen so quickly we probably don't have time to notice anything strange. What does Penny think?'

'I haven't had a chance to talk to her, we don't seem to connect when she's on nights, and she's going on leave soon, so she's been pretty busy.' It was only when she said it that Laura realised just how soon Penny was going to leave. 'It's tomorrow or the day after, I think.'

'We should try to get together before she goes, but she may not have time,' commented Jane. 'I'm pretty tied up, anyway.'

She was to be married in a few weeks, and with something of a relief, for it took her mind off the vague and formless apprehension she had been feeling, Laura asked her friend about the wedding plans, and they discussed this through the remainder of the meal.

'Just make sure both you and Jeff are off on the right day,' said Jane, refilling her coffee cup. 'We must have our best man and our bridesmaid there, after all—after Stewart and me, you and Jeff are the most important people.' For a moment, her clear blue eyes met Laura's. 'I did think, at one time, we might have been planning a double wedding.'

Laura felt warm colour in her cheeks.

'You know Jeff and me,' she replied lightly. 'We've been friends for so long there isn't any rush about—taking things any further. Besides, remember what the three of us always said—never marry a doctor! At least you've had the sense to choose a lawyer instead, and Penny's love-life changes so quickly we can't keep up with it!'

She looked at her watch.

'Time I was back on the ward,' she said, standing up. 'Operating day today—we've got to be ready for the doctors' round. See you, Jane. 'Bye!'

She hurried along the corridor, looked at the lift, and decided that walking up two flights of stairs would be quicker. Already she was mentally reviewing the afternoon's work. Her post-operative patients all needed careful monitoring. She checked the drips that had been set up, adjusted a drain, and dealt with a catheter problem—remembering, always, how she had felt as a student nurse, and then as a staff nurse, hoping always to be given responsibility and experience, but at the same time, grateful for Sister's ever-watchful eye in the background. She stood by patiently, while her second-year nurse adjusted a difficult drip, and she hoped she had succeeded in letting the girl know that she was completely confident of her ability to do it.

It was during the doctors' rounds later that she was again conscious of that strange tension. Her doctors were careful and they were conscientious, but yet—she had the feeling, somehow, that their thoughts were not entirely on her ward, and her patients.

It was the following day that she heard the first mention of the farmer's wife who had been brought in from somewhere near Saldanha Bay.

'They're not sure whether she has enteritis, or a bleeding ulcer, or what,' one of the nurses coming on night duty remarked fairly casually. 'Apparently her own doctor thought she had 'flu. There's been so much of it around even this early in winter, but then he wasn't too happy about her condition, so he had her brought in here. No, I haven't seen her, I just heard someone talking about her. I don't know why there's so much interest, we get enough bleeding ulcers around not to get overly excited about another one.'

'Speaking about ulcers,' said Laura, lifting one of the charts from the folder on the desk, 'we're not too happy about Mrs Fowler in Six—she had a duodenal removed today, and her blood pressure is very low. Dr Brown is at this number if you need to call him. See you in the morning.'

'Have a nice evening,' the Night Sister called, as she reached the door. 'Doing anything special?'

'Depends,' Laura replied, 'on how human I feel after I've bathed and changed. And on whether Jeff is on call.'

There was a message from Jeff waiting for her, to tell her that he wasn't on call, and the evening was theirs. Laura, who had come off duty feeling she wouldn't have been too disappointed to spend the evening lazily with a book, bathed and changed a little reluctantly.

But by the time she took the lift down to the entrance hall of the Nurses' Home, to see Jeff Sheldon waiting for her, she found she was rather looking forward to doing something different. It was always fun, going out with Jeff.

'Hi, Dr Sheldon,' she said, hurrying across to him. 'Busy day?'

His lips brushed her cheeks.

'You ever hear any doctor admit he hasn't had a busy day?' Jeff returned, smiling down at her. 'You too, I'm sure. Anything special you want to do, Laura?' And when she shook her head, 'Then I thought we'd go across to Sea Point, maybe have a walk, then have something to eat. All right with you?'

'I'd love that,' Laura told him, pleased. 'A good walk and some sea air will be marvellous.'

They talked, easily and casually, about their work, about Jane and Stewart's wedding, as Jeff drove over the freeway high above the lights of Cape Town, and Laura felt the last of the day's tensions ease away. By the time Jeff parked his car right beside the sea, and handed her her thick jersey, the hospital seemed farther away than just the other side of the city.

'It's always so nice here,' she murmured, pulling her jersey on. 'Even in winter, when the rest of Cape Town can be pretty miserable, it's worth coming over. Can we walk down to the lighthouse, Jeff?'

They walked along beside the sea, sometimes stopping to look at the waves thundering on to the shore, sometimes looking at the lights of ships far out at sea.

'The mist is coming in,' Jeff commented. 'The old foghorn's busy already.'

They listened to the mournful sound of the foghorn giving its warning.

'I've sometimes thought I'd like to work at the Somerset,' said Laura, mentioning the big hospital a little beyond the lighthouse. 'Then I could live right here beside the sea—but when I think of the foghorn I change my mind! Just imagine hearing that all through the night!'

They turned to walk back towards the bright lights of Sea Point, and Jeff took her hand in his, lightly, easily. Just as his kiss, a little later, before they left the seclusion of the path beside the sea, was light, casual, pleasant.

'Do you remember when you were a student nurse, and I was a fourth-year medic? I said then, That's the girl I'm going to marry,' Jeff told her, taking her hand again as they walked on.

'You did not,' Laura retorted laughing. 'Whatever the intentions of a fourth-year medic, I'd take a bet marriage doesn't enter into them!'

'Cross my heart,' he assured her dramatically. 'Ask any of the fellows. That's the girl I'm going to marry, I said—that lovely and innocent creature in virginal white.'

'With a bedpan to match in her hand,' she reminded him. 'Which I almost dropped in my agitation at meeting a whole group of medical students!'

She looked up at him.

'I'm starving,' she told him. 'All this fresh air after a hard day's work.'

Jeff sighed.

'No hard-up young doctor should have a nurse for a girl-friend—nurses are always hungry! Pizza do you?'

'Pizza will be fine,' Laura replied.

They walked along the busy main street until they came to their favourite Pizza Den, and after careful consideration, each ordered a different pizza, so that they could share.

It was only when they were almost ready to leave, and finishing the last of the pot of coffee Jeff had ordered, that Laura remembered she had meant to ask Jeff about the patient from Saldanha Bay.

'Have you heard about the woman from Saldanha Bay?' she asked him.

'Yes, I have,' he said, and it was only later that she thought there had been a moment's hesitation.

She looked at him, a little surprised that he hadn't said any more.

'Well, why is everyone so interested in her?' she asked him.

He seemed to be concentrating on stirring his coffee.

'The clinical picture is a little strange,' he said carefully.

Perhaps, Laura thought later, looking back, perhaps that was the moment when things began to fall into place.

The next day she heard the farmer's wife had been moved from Medical to a small isolation ward. After that, there was no doubt at all about the growing strain around the hospital, and the rumours became much more specific.

'I heard,' Jane told her confidentially. 'that there's a remote possibility it might be one of the haemorrhagic fevers. Lassa—Congo-Crimean—Green Monkey. Apparently that Virology Institute has been asked to do blood samples in their top-secret lab.'

Laura had heard much the same, but they decided that the possibility was remote, for there had been only two victims of heamorrhagic fevers in all of South Africa in recent years, one of them an Australian girl who had travelled from Zimbabwe, and the other a boy who had been bitten by an infected tick.

But remote possibility or not, by another day, the farmer's wife was in strict isolation, and the latest news was that until a positive result could be reached from the blood tests, she was to be treated as if she did indeed have a highly contagious, very dangerous and almost unknown disease.

The next day, the hospital held a press conference, for there had been increasing speculation in the recent newspapers, and even a report that the Virology Institute had been contacted.

Half an hour before the press conference, the nursing staff on each ward were told what everyone in fact knew by then—that although there was as yet no positive identification of the disease, there was no doubt that Mrs Elize Marais was suffering from a haemorrhagic fever, and anyone who had been in contact with her was being kept in isolation. An isolation ward had been set up in Block B, with an intensive care unit, and arrangements were being made to increase the staff if this became necessary.

There was, it was emphasised, no cause for any panic, the situation was under control.

But—an intensive care unit, Laura thought soberly. That must mean that if the farmer's wife wasn't already extremely ill, it was expected that she might become so.

Half an hour before Laura was due to go off duty, she was told that Miss Reston, the Assistant Matron, wanted to see her. Curious, and in spite of a clear conscience a little apprehensive, she made her way to Miss Reston's office.

'Sister Kent,' Miss Reston greeted her, and Laura saw that her folder lay open on the desk. 'Sit down,

Sister.' For a moment, her grey eyes met Laura's steadily, and Laura saw that the older woman was tired—tired and worried. 'You may have guessed what I'm going to ask you, Sister,' she went on quietly. 'You know what the situation is, and you've heard about the isolation ward in Block B. I know you've had no experience of barrier nursing, other than theoretical, and certainly not of nursing a disease as little known as this.'

She paused, and Laura asked, tentatively, if there had been a positive identification yet.

'Not yet,' the older woman replied, and she took off her glasses and rubbed her eyes. 'But we're assuming the worst—a Congo-Crimean fever. You will realise, Sister, that with something as little known as this, there's the possibility of infection to the nursing staff, even with the greatest care. That's why you have the right to refuse.' She smiled, but the smile didn't reach her eyes. 'I may as well be honest with you, and tell you that of the three other Sisters I've spoken to, two have refused. Do you need time to think about this? I can give you until tomorrow morning.'

Laura shook her head.

'I don't need time,' she said steadily. 'How soon do you need me in Block B, Matron?'

For a moment the older woman's eyes held hers. Then, as if satisfied, she nodded.

'Right away, Sister,' she said briskly. 'I know you're supposed to be going off duty now, but we need you to report to Block B within two hours, if possible.' And answering Laura's unspoken question, 'I would, of course, have given you until tomorrow, but—how quickly can you pack up the essentials you need? Don't worry about clearing your room in the Nurses' Home, take as little as possible.'

The next two hours were a whirl of activity for Laura—packing a suitcase, leaving a note to tell Jane, who was still on duty, where she was going, phoning her mother, and leaving a message at the doctors' bungalow for Jeff.

At last, with her suitcase in her hand, she stood at the door of the Sisters' flat she and Jane shared, and for the first time since leaving Matron's office she had a moment to think of this step into the unknown that she was taking. As she was closing the door, the phone rang. Laura hesitated, but lifted the receiver.

'Laura?' said Jeff brusquely. 'I've just got your message. Look, I have no right to tell you what to do, but shouldn't you think about this?'

'Someone has to do it,' Laura pointed out reasonably. 'And it will be good experience, Jeff.'

For a moment there was silence, and she could picture him frowning, his blue eyes clouded.

'I could get off for half an hour,' he said at last. 'We could at least have a quick coffee.'

'Sorry, Jeff,' she said, with regret. 'I should be there now, I must go. 'Bye.'

Suddenly, unaccountably, she knew that she didn't want to see Jeff now, she wanted to get right into whatever awaited her in Block B.

'Take care, Laura,' said Jeff, surprisingly, and there was something in his voice that made her put the receiver down slowly. Some time before too long, she was going to have to do some thinking about Jeff and herself, she knew that. Their friendship, their easy, undemanding relationship had lasted for a long time, but she had sensed, recently, that Jeff was less happy than she was about this. Perhaps, she thought reluctantly, this is one of the reasons I'm happy to go off to Block B, where I won't see him on the ward.

She closed the door then, and picked up her suitcase and went along to the lift. There was a connecting passage to Block B, but to her surprise she found that it had been closed, and she had to walk across the central lawn instead.

Block B, like the other huge buildings, had big glass doors that were usually kept open, but today there was only the small side door open. Laura went inside, and found that the reception desk had been moved as close to the door as possible.

'Big changes, George,' she said, as the hospital porter looked up and smiled a greeting. 'Where am I supposed to go?'

'You'll have to wait here, Sister,' the porter told her, 'until your identity tag comes. The new fellow says no one's to get in without their tag, and yours isn't here yet.'

Laura put her suitcase down.

'A bit ridiculous, surely,' she said impatiently, 'when I was told to be here at this time.'

George shrugged.

'Orders, Sister,' he replied. 'They've just got this big fellow here from Johannesburg, this expert, and what he says goes.'

She turned and looked back across the administration block, hoping to see a messenger bringing this 'necessary identification tag'.

Afterwards, she was to realise that her own behaviour was a reaction to the apprehension and anxiety she was already feeling. If she hadn't been feeling extremely concerned at what Matron had told her—if there hadn't been the growing certainty that the whole situation was extremely serious—

But she was concerned, she was anxious, she was apprehensive. And so she tried to hide her own feelings, from herself and from anyone else, by speaking lightly, carelessly. Thoughtlessly, she realised, afterwards.

'For goodness' sake, I hope we're not all going to be behaving as if we're in a third-rate pseudo-medical film!' she exclaimed. 'This is all a bit heavy handed. Who is this expert, anyway?'

She saw the porter's eyes looking behind her.

'Heavy-handed, perhaps, Sister, but necessary. My orders, I'm afraid.'

Laura swung round to look at the big dark man she hadn't heard coming along the corridor. He stood towering above her, his dark eyes cold.

'I think, Sister,' he went on evenly, 'you and I had better have a talk right away, so that you can understand exactly what the position is. Come into my office, please.'

He turned and walked away.

Laura picked up her suitcase and followed him, wishing with all her heart that she hadn't spoken as she had, but at the same time, furious with this man and his high-handed attitude.

Whoever you are, Mr Big Doctor, she said silently, I don't think we're going to get on, you and I!

CHAPTER TWO

'I'M sorry, Doctor,' Laura said stiffly, her head held high, 'I shouldn't have said that.'

'No, Sister, you shouldn't,' the big man returned evenly.

Later, she was to hear his voice described by one of the young nurses as a warm, dark-brown voice, straight from the heather. But there was nothing warm in it at that moment.

He didn't introduce himself, but his name was on his name tag: Dr David Mackay.

'You obviously have no experience of Congo-type haemorrhagic fevers, Sister,' he said, standing on one side of the desk and making no suggestion that Laura should sit down. 'I suggest you read up your textbooks so that you can appreciate that we're dealing with a killer disease. I can assure you that this is not a third-rate pseudo-medical film, it's a very real situation, and I would advise you to treat it with less levity.'

Laura felt the colour drain from her face.

'I didn't—I shouldn't—' she faltered.

'No, you didn't, and you shouldn't,' Dr Mackay agreed, with no amusement in his voice or in his eyes. 'We're in a crisis situation, Sister, and don't forget it.' He nodded curtly. 'That will be all.'

Dismissed, Laura lifted her suitcase and walked back along the corridor.

'Here's your tag come now, Sister,' the porter told her. 'You can go in.'

Laura unpinned her old tag and put on the new one, and for a moment, absurdly, she wondered if it was too late, if she couldn't turn now, go back to Miss Reston and say that she had changed her mind, she didn't want to work in Block B.

But she knew that she couldn't do that, just because a high-handed doctor had given her the worst dressing-down she had had since she was a student nurse.

'I just have to work with him,' she told herself firmly. 'It doesn't matter how much I dislike him.'

She found her room, and the duty list, and tired as she was, it was something of a relief to see that she had been put on night duty, and she would have to have something to eat right away, and then report to the ward.

'Sorry to do this to you, Sister Kent,' the Senior Sister said when she went on duty. 'I've asked Jill Derry to stay on a bit later, so that I can take you around and give you a brief rundown—Dr Mackay has called a staff conference for tomorrow morning, and I'm afraid you'll have to attend, even after being on night duty. Now, we're beyond mask technique here, this is what you will wear each time you go into the isolation ward, or the intensive care unit. We have Mrs Marais in intensive care now, and the contacts are in isolation.'

The gowns and the hoods, with clear plastic visors, looked like something out of a science fiction film. And there was a Vickers respirator on a trolley.

'A spare,' Sister Retief said tersely. 'Mrs Marais is on one.'

Laura looked from the equipment she would be using, to the protective clothing, and she thought, soberly, that Dr Mackay had been right: this was indeed a crisis situation.

'This Dr Mackay,' she said casually, as she and the older Sister went back along the corridor, 'who is he, and why is he here?'

'I don't know a great deal about him,' Sister Retief replied. 'I believe he left Scotland a few years ago, and did a great deal of work on Lassa fever in Kinshasa, and then he went to Johannesburg, to the Virology Institute. Apparently in the whole country he's the doctor with the best working knowledge of haemorrhagic fevers, so we're lucky to have him.'

They sat down together in the duty room, and Laura listened to her instructions for the night nursing of her patient.

'You'll have a staff nurse with you,' Sister Retief told her. 'Each of you will have the usual breaks, and during the time only one nurse is on duty, you're to contact Dr Mackay himself if there is any change in the patient's condition. Any change at all. At any other time, one nurse will remain with the patient, and the other will come out of the intensive care unit and then report. At the moment, your nursing consists mostly of providing symptomatic relief, apart from constant monitoring of the respirator, and the observations for drug sensitivity.'

It was strange, seeing herself and her staff nurse in their spaceman suits, and Laura couldn't help thinking that necessary as this was, it would only emphasise to their patient how serious her condition was. But once they were in the intensive care unit, she saw that Mrs Marais was in fact too ill to take in much at all, and certainly too ill to be caused any distress by the protective clothing worn by her nurses.

It was a long, tiring night's duty. Not that there was so much to be done, but she had to be alert every moment, conscious of the slightest change. Once, when

her staff nurse was off for a tea break, Laura turned to
see a tall figure, protectively gowned and hooded,
coming in. David Mackay's gloved hand beckoned to
her, and she joined him at the far side of the room.

'I'd like to see your report, Sister,' he said, his voice
low, and muffled by the visor.

Silently, Laura handed him the chart and the hourly
reports, and stood waiting as he studied them. Then,
with a nod, he handed them back to her and went over
to examine the woman in the bed. Laura, moving over
as well, was surprised to hear him talking to Mrs Marais.

'You're not just feeling very great, Mrs Marais,' he
said, and even distorted by the mask, she could hear
the sympathy and the warmth in his voice. 'I'm having
something sent from America that I hope will be help-
ing you—perhaps tomorrow it will be here. I'm going
now, but Sister Kent is here with you.'

At the door, he looked down at Laura.

'I don't think she's able to take in much,' he said, his
voice so low that Laura could barely hear it. 'But you
never know. I like to give a patient the benefit of the
doubt, every time, and a word of sympathy and reassurance never goes amiss. Thank you, Sister, you're
doing fine.'

It was a point of view Laura liked, one she held herself, and it threw her a little to hear it expressed by this
man. It made him, she thought with reluctance, something more than she had thought.

And the next day, that reluctant admiration for
David Mackay as a doctor grew even more, as she sat
with the rest of the staff of Block B listening to him
outlining the situation.

'Right, that takes care of what we have to do to assist
in identifying the etiologic agent, and establishing the

diagnosis,' he said briskly. 'We've dealt with the technical aspects of that, and of controlling infection in the patient, and in preventing any spread of infection. My rules are very specific, and there will be no deviation from them. But there is another aspect of our nursing care. It applies to Mrs Marais, ill as she is, and showing as few signs of understanding as she does, and it will apply to any further patients, as well as to the contacts who are now in isolation. We must recognise the loneliness of the isolated patient, and we must do what we can to relieve the inevitable anxiety and depression. Our responsibility goes beyond the specific physical care, and I want us all to remember that.' He looked around the room and smiled. 'Thank you.'

Laura picked up the notes she had made and went out of the room with the girl who had been her staff nurse through the night on duty.

'He's quite something, isn't he?' the younger girl said, with enthusiasm. 'Those dark eyes, and that lovely Scottish voice!'

Laura shrugged.

'He seems to know what he's talking about,' she replied carefully.

'I could listen to him reading the telephone directory, with that accent,' Nurse Evans said dreamily.

She looked around, making sure there was no one near them.

'We were talking about him in the duty room yesterday,' she said, her voice low. 'I said surely he must be married, or at least well and truly booked—I mean, that voice, and although he's got too strong a face to be called tall, dark and handsome, he's certainly tall and dark, and kind of rugged, and although he doesn't smile much, I can just imagine—'

In spite of herself, Laura smiled.

'Beth, I don't have time to stand and listen to you singing Dr Mackay's praises—I'm off duty now, I want to eat, and bath and sleep!'

'But it's much more interesting than that,' Beth Evans assured her. 'You know Mary Peters in Theatre? Well, apparently her cousin, who was a paediatric nurse at Johannesburg Gen., had been going steady with our Dr Mackay for ages—well, a long time anyway. Then suddenly they broke up, and apparently Sandra Peters took it so badly she resigned and went to work in a clinic in New York. Her family was very upset, I hear.'

'You hear too much,' Laura said crisply. 'Really, Beth, Dr Mackay's private life is no concern of ours.'

But it did, she couldn't help thinking, confirm her immediate dislike of the man. Obviously he had behaved as arrogantly to this girl as he had behaved to her. Not that it mattered, of course. As far as she was concerned, she reminded herself, he was nothing more than the competent and knowledgeable doctor in charge of a difficult situation.

And that he undoubtedly was. Each time she came in contact with him, she was impressed by him, in a purely professional sense. The staff being fairly small, that happened more often that it would have in other circumstances, and perhaps, too, the unusual aspect of this case made for a closeness and a camaraderie that grew exceptionally quickly. After only three days in Block B, Laura felt, somehow, that she had been working there for months.

A new and untested anti-viral drug had arrived from America and had been given to Mrs Marais, but there was little improvement in her condition. The virology unit, after intensive research, had announced that this was indeed a Congo-type fever, and that Mrs Marais had been infected by a fever-carrying tick. All tick-bites were to be reported to a doctor, and the newspapers carried large illustrations of what was known as the 'bont-legged' tick. So far, none of the contacts showed signs of developing the disease, but Dr Mackay reminded his staff constantly that this did not mean they were in the clear. Not yet.

Off duty one afternoon, and prevented by the regulations from going away from Block B, Laura changed into jeans and a blue shirt and took her book down to the small enclosed garden. The sun, even now in early winter, was warm, and she found her eyes closing, and the book slipping from her hands.

She couldn't have been asleep for long, but somehow she knew, before she opened her eyes, that she wasn't alone. David Mackay was sitting on the deckchair next to hers. There was a copy of the morning paper in his hands, but he was asleep.

And like that, with dark lashes on the brown of his cheeks, his dark hair rumpled, his mouth relaxed, he looked younger. More—vulnerable, Laura found herself thinking involuntarily. Defenceless, almost. And very tired.

Her thoughts surprised her, and she told herself hastily that she was tired too, that it was only because she wasn't fully awake that she had allowed herself to think of him with some sympathy, instead of with her usual reaction to him.

He must have sat there, as she was doing now, and looked at her as she slept, she realised. And there was something extremely disturbing in that realisation, in the thought of David Mackay sitting here studying her, perhaps deciding, as she had done about him, that she looked more vulnerable when she was asleep.

Her own thoughts, running away in this ridiculous fashion, brought a reluctant smile to Laura's lips. As if David Mackay would do more than give a cursory glance at a sleeping nurse, wish there was somewhere else to go and sit, and then open his newspaper, and promptly fall asleep. And while he's asleep, I shall just disappear, Laura thought.

But his sleep must have been very light, for when she moved he opened his eyes, immediately awake.

'I'm sorry,' Laura said stiffly, awkwardly, 'I didn't mean to disturb you.'

To her surprise, he smiled, a little diffidently.

'Don't rush off,' he said. 'I was hoping to have the chance of a few words with you.'

'I don't really think there's any need for that,' she replied coolly. 'I understand the situation now.'

'But I disagree, Sister Laura Kent,' he said pleasantly. 'I feel that you and I got off on the wrong foot the other day, because I happened to overhear what you said. Please believe me, I have no intention of holding a rather thoughtless remark against you, and I hope you won't be holding it against me that I did happen to overhear. Now, could we not just be forgetting the whole thing?'

'It's of no importance, really,' Laura replied, somewhat thrown by his frankness.

David Mackay sat up straight, his dark eyes holding hers.

'It is important, Laura—do you mind? We're a small team here, and I think it is very likely that there will be difficult times ahead of us. I don't want any bad feelings in my team. So—it is important.'

He was very close to her. Suddenly, ridiculously, Laura felt breathless, stifled. She moved, and her book fell. As she reached for it, David Mackay reached for it as well, and his hand covered hers on the book.

Afterwards, she told herself that it was only for a moment, and it was only because of the circumstances that she felt so strange. But it seemed to her that the whole world narrowed to herself and this man, and his hand covering hers, his face very close to hers, and a silence filled only with the unsteady thudding of her heart.

Slowly she drew her hand out from under his, and hoped he hadn't seen that she was trembling.

'Laura?' he said softly.

She turned away and put the book into her shoulder bag.

'I'm sorry, Dr Mackay,' she replied, not looking at him, her voice light, bright. 'Of course you're right, and if I've made things difficult in any way, I do apologise.' Somehow she managed to smile. 'Now, if you don't mind, I must go.'

He stood up as well, and she wondered if she was imagining that there was a look of disappointment in his eyes.

'Do go on with your newspaper, you'll find we're all mentioned in it,' she said quickly.

She walked away then, but although she didn't turn round, she knew he stood watching her until she went round the corner. Back in her room, she changed into her uniform, brushed her hair and pinned it up. Her cheeks were flushed, she saw—even this winter sun had been warm.

He's quite right, she told herself sensibly, we can't afford bad feelings in a small team, so I'll regard him as nothing more than the very competent doctor I'm working for.

And she pushed away the blood-tingling memory of that moment in the garden, when she had been able to regard him only as a man she felt a strong and very physical attraction to.

This should be another long and quiet night, she told herself briskly, wondering if there had been any change in Mrs Marais' condition, for the night before Laura had felt that the farmer's wife was barely holding her own. The anti-viral drug, although not giving any dramatic results, did seem to be preventing any further deterioration.

But when she had changed into her protective clothing for the intensive care unit, she found David Mackay waiting for her in the small outer room. He too was gowned ready to go in, and his helmet was in his hand. He looked at Laura and her staff nurse, and his face was bleak.

'Mrs Marais has been given a transfusion, but her condition has deteriorated,' he told them quietly. 'I shall be here all the night, Sister Kent.'

Laura waited, somehow knowing that there was more.

'We have another patient in the other intensive care room,' he went on. 'A staff nurse from Block A. She thought she had 'flu, and it was only when she haemorrhaged that she was sent here. She—is very ill indeed.'

He had turned away, but Laura took a step after him.

'Dr Mackay?'

He swung round.

'This staff nurse,' Laura asked him, 'is she one of the contacts we had in isolation?'

For a long time, it seemed, the big doctor looked down at her.

'No,' he said at last, wearily. 'No, she isn't. The really frightening aspect of this is that this nurse has not been in direct contact with Mrs Marais at all. And this could change a great many things for the worse.'

CHAPTER THREE

JUST after four in the morning, their patient died.

Laura and David Mackay were with her, and although both of them had known since midnight that it was only a matter of time, and that nothing could be done, neither of them had moved from her side.

David Mackay stood up and turned the respirator off. Through the plastic mask Laura could see the lines of strain on his face, and in spite of everything she felt about this man, she couldn't help being sorry for him, for she could see how it affected him, that all his skill and his knowledge had not succeeded in saving this woman.

Outside, his mask in his hand, he turned to her.

'I'm sure I don't have to remind you, Sister, to see that your staff nurse follows to the letter the procedure I've outlined for disinfecting after isolation,' he said. 'Everything needed for the other patient is, as you know, being kept entirely separate.' For a moment, his eyes held hers. 'You will also, please, see that this room is prepared for any other admission we may have to make.'

'I'll see to that, Dr Mackay,' Laura replied, and went through to give instructions to the staff nurse. When she came back, David Mackay was still standing as she had left him, his mask in his hand.

'Would you like a cup of coffee, Dr Mackay?' she asked him.

It was a moment before he answered.

'Yes, thank you, Sister, I certainly would,' he said, and he followed her into the tiny kitchen adjoining the intensive care unit.

'We didn't get her soon enough, of course, that was the biggest problem,' he said, as much to himself as to her, as she put a mug of steaming coffee down in front of him. 'Thanks, Sister.'

Laura hesitated, but only for a moment, before she sat down on the other side of the table with her own coffee.

'What about the other patient in isolation?' she asked him quietly. 'Staff Nurse Abbott—Susan Abbott.'

'You know her?' he asked, but Laura shook her head.

'She's a very sick girl—very sick indeed,' David Mackay said carefully. 'As you know, I'm giving her the works, I'm hitting this with every darned thing— the new anti-viral drug, anti-serum we've kept from any patients who've survived any Congo-type fever, Interferon. Her condition is stable, her breathing is better than Mrs Marais' was when I saw her first, and I'm not as worried about her vital functions. But having said that, I have to say too that that situation could change and deteriorate rapidly. The one thing I do know about haemorrhagic fevers is that I don't know enough.' He put his cup down and looked at her. 'You're tired, Sister Kent,' he said, unexpectedly. 'I'm going to suggest that you sleep for a day and a night, and then have a spell out of intensive care, supervising the people we have in isolation.'

The concern in his eyes shook Laura. She felt, in some way that she didn't want to examine too closely, that this man had no right to behave with kindness and consideration, no right to behave in any way that didn't fit with what she thought she knew of him.

'I'm all right, Dr Mackay,' she said, more brusquely than she had intended to. 'It seems a pity to waste the experience I've had in here, though, whether I'm on nights or days.'

'Aye, that is so,' David Mackay agreed. 'But you'll find, Sister, that the people who are being kept in isolation are in need of your care and your experience too, in a different way.' He stood up. 'Thank you for the coffee, Sister, and—thank you for all you have done here.'

She went with him to the door, and as he was going out he turned and looked, for a moment, as if he was going to say something else. To her chagrin, Laura felt warm colour flood her cheeks.

'You look tired too, Dr Mackay,' she said quickly.

'I haven't the time to be tired,' he replied, 'for now that Nurse Abbott has contracted the disease, and her never having been in direct contact with the patient, I have a great deal of thinking and organising to do. Put simply, it means, as I'm sure you're aware, that we now have to consider contacts who were not even direct contacts, and at an earlier stage than we've been working on. So you see, I have no time to be tired.'

When he had gone, Laura went back to help her staff nurse with the painstaking disinfecting procedure. Terminal cleaning, her textbook called it, she remembered bleakly.

Rather to her own surprise, she did sleep for a good part of the day, and having established that she was to go on day duty, she managed to have a good night's sleep as well.

David Mackay, she found when she went on duty, had left instructions that she was to spend the day working with the people who were being kept in isolation. There were nine of them, dating from the time Mrs Marais' disease had been judged to be infectious, although this would change now, because of the new admission, the young nurse lying in intensive care. None of these people were ill, or even showing any signs of the fever developing, but they had to be checked and monitored under carefully supervised barrier nursing conditions.

'Seems a bit unnecessary, when there isn't a raised temperature or a 'fluey sign among the lot of them,' one of the nurses murmured to Laura as they sterilised yet another batch of used linen.

'Protective isolation,' Laura reminded her. 'Containing the disease is as important as curing it.' She smiled. 'Sorry I sound stuffy, but it is important.'

She found that David Mackay had been right about the people in isolation becoming anxious and depressed and lonely, and she spent a considerable amount of time reassuring Mrs Marais' sister, who had come to Cape Town in the ambulance with her, and who had in fact been her only visitor in the hospital, that she was not developing the disease as well.

'You see, Sister,' she said tearfully, 'Elize thought it was 'flu she had, she just felt a little shivery at first. And now she's gone, just like that, and I have to be kept here. And—and I think I feel just the same, just like the start of 'flu too.'

'Your temperature is normal, Mrs Venter,' Laura reminded her, fairly firmly. 'And we're checking regularly, so we'll know if there's any change at all. But time does hang heavily, doesn't it, and you have too much time to think. Now, what about the arrangements you were making by telephone, for your sister's family? Did you get something fixed up? And what about your own family?'

The woman nodded, and began to tell Laura that she had asked a cousin to take Mrs Marais' two children, and her own three, and look after them.

'They have a big old farmhouse, you see, and Betty has plenty of room, and the children all go to the same school. It will relieve Johan's mind, to know that the children are being looked after.'

And it's helped you, just a little, Laura thought, to have something to think about, even just making these arrangements.

She stayed a little longer, asking about Mrs Venter's children, listening while her patient spoke about when she and her sister were children.

'We've never been apart for long, Elize and I,' she said sadly. 'There's only a year between us, and we did everything together. And both of us being married to farmers kept us close. That's why I came with her, instead of Johan—it isn't easy for a farmer, getting away. And now it's just as well he didn't come, just as well I was the one to be in contact with Elize, and kept here.'

She turned her head away, but not before Laura had seen slow tears running down her cheeks.

'I'll miss her so much,' she whispered. And Laura, longing to put her arms around the woman, to try to comfort her just a little, knew she could not. After a moment Marie Venter tried to smile. 'Thank you, Sister, for being here,' she said quietly.

The other isolation contacts, without the same personal tie with the woman who had died, were less hard to deal with. Boredom and loneliness were their chief problems, and although some did show signs of anxiety about whether they might have contracted the disease, in the main Laura found a faith in the medical team looking after them that touched her deeply.

She had got into the habit of going out into the small enclosed garden any time she was off duty, for the lack of fresh air and exercise bothered her. Since that warm, sunny afternoon, she hadn't seen David Mackay there, but now, when she opened the door and went outside, she saw, in the shade of the big tree, a man in a white coat.

Instinctively she turned away, but not quickly enough, for the man turned as well.

But it wasn't David Mackay, it was Jeff.

'What are you doing here, Jeff?' asked Laura, astonished.

He smiled and came towards her, taking both her hands in his.

'I came to see you, of course. Pulled a few strings, but after all, you girls aren't infectious, and I have no intention of going near any of your patients.'

He looked down at her.

'Laura, love,' he said soberly, 'I wish you hadn't said you'd do this. I wasn't happy about it before, and now, with one death, and another possible—I've talked to Miss Reston, Laura, and she says you can leave Block B if you want to.'

Laura shook her head.

'I wouldn't think of it, Jeff,' she told him with certainty. 'I've packed a lot of experience into this short time, and I'm useful to the team now. I'm not leaving.'

His hands were still holding both of hers, and she tried to free herself, but he held her more firmly.

'I've been doing a lot of thinking in these last few days, Laura,' he said, and there was something disturbing in his blue eyes, something new. 'We've known each other a long time, we've gone around together, we've had fun, and I think I've been in danger of taking you for granted. But not any more, not after this. Things are going to change, Laura, starting now.'

Before she could even try to stop him, he took her in his arms and kissed her, a kiss unlike any other kiss he had ever given her. And it was only later that Laura realised that there had been no response in her, to the urgency of his kiss, nothing but a longing to free herself.

'No, Jeff—no!'

She managed to turn her head away, and he released her.

'This is no time to be thinking of ourselves,' she said, breathless from his kiss. And angry, now.

He smiled.

'Perhaps not,' he agreed, unrepentant. 'But I wanted to let you know how I felt.'

You certainly managed to do that, Laura thought, trying to find her lost sense of humour.

'I think you'd better go, Jeff,' she told him firmly. 'I'm sure you shouldn't be here.'

'Probably not,' he agreed, 'but George and I are old friends.'

'You'll get George into trouble,' she warned, 'not to mention me.'

Without waiting for any reply, she turned to go back inside.

David Mackay was at the door, his dark brows drawn down, his eyes cold and remote. How long had he been there? Laura wondered frantically.

'Dr Sheldon, I believe?' David Mackay asked frostily. 'I'm afraid we're not encouraging visits, even from hospital staff.'

Jeff smiled, not at all put out.

'Well, I may be doing more than visiting, I'm on your reserve list if you need to increase your team, Dr

Mackay,' he returned. 'But in any case, I came to see my fiancée, and check that she's all right. Goodbye, Laura love.'

His lips brushed hers, and he was gone, with a jaunty wave. Laura and David Mackay were left staring at each other, both, Laura realised, equally taken aback.

'I'll thank you, Sister Kent,' said David Mackay, recovering first, his Scottish accent more pronounced than usual, 'to remind your fiancé that I am the one who makes the rules here in Block B, and I'll be instructing George to let no one in without my express permission.'

'Certainly, Dr Mackay,' Laura replied, not quite steadily. And then, realising the implication of what she had said, she turned to follow him as he strode along the corridor.

'Dr Mackay—' she began breathlessly, her hand on his arm.

He stopped, and looked down at her.

'Dr Sheldon isn't my fiancé. I mean, we're not engaged or anything, I don't know why he said that,' she said, her words tumbling over each other as his dark eyes looked down at her.

'No?' he returned, after a moment, his eyebrows raised. 'You surprise me, Sister Kent. The young man was certainly behaving as if the two of you knew each other very well. Very well indeed. But I will not be interfering in your private life, as long as *you* don't let it interfere with my orders here in Block B.'

And without giving her a chance to say anything more, he walked away, his white coat flying, his dark head high, leaving Laura staring helplessly after him.

Although why should I care what David Mackay thinks of me, she asked herself, considering the fact that my opinion of him is certainly not of the highest!

But in spite of that, the thought of facing the condemnation in the Scottish doctor's eyes time after time dismayed her more than she would have thought possible.

She should, of course, have known better than that, she realised after their first meeting in the duty room at the isolation ward, for there was nothing but professional detachment in the way David Mackay spoke to her—courteous, polite, and completely professional, as he discussed with her the changes he wanted made in the keeping of charts. He is, Laura thought unwillingly, as she had come to think more and more often, a very good doctor indeed.

That evening she phoned her mother, knowing that as a nurse herself, she would look at the situation in the hospital sensibly, but knowing, too, that she would appreciate the reassurance from Laura that she herself was all right. She was more than a little taken aback to hear from her mother that Jeff had looked in to see them, to express his concern about Laura working in Block B.

'What did you say to him?' she asked her mother carefully.

Her mother's reply was equally careful.

'I told him we would obviously be happier to see you out of there, but you were old enough to make your own decisions. Right?'

'Right,' Laura agreed. 'Sorry, Mum, I didn't mean to sound short, but it's nothing to do with Jeff.'

And I wish he'd realise that, she thought, as she said goodbye and put the receiver down.

The next day there was a message for her to go and see Dr Mackay. Laura's heart sank. If Jeff had been doing some more interfering—

'Sit down, Sister Kent,' said David Mackay, without looking up from the notes on his desk.

Laura sat down, her legs neatly crossed at the ankles, her hands folded in her lap, waiting.

'You're a friend of Sister Harding—Penny Harding—I believe?' he went on, so unexpectedly that Laura forgot her apprehensions about Jeff.

'Yes, I am,' she replied, surprised.

His eyes met hers.

'Sister Harding was on night duty in Medical when Mrs Marais was brought in,' he said evenly. 'She wasn't included in the list of possible contacts until we had to re-think this, and work on the assumption that Mrs Marais was infectious at an earlier stage than we thought. Now we've followed up any other possible contact at that stage, but Sister Harding has gone on leave, and Miss Reston suggested you might know where she is, as she has left no information at the Nurses' Home. We do know that she hasn't gone to her home, and they can't help either—apparently she's fairly casual.'

Laura sat back, collecting her thoughts.

'No, she changed her plans at the last minute,' she told him. 'She was going to her sister in Durban, but her sister had to go away unexpectedly. I'm not sure exactly where Penny has gone, but another friend of ours works at a small convalescent home in the Drakensberg, and Penny was talking about ringing Irene to see if she could go there.' She hesitated. 'She is a little casual—it doesn't bother her folks or her friends.'

David Mackay lifted his pen.

'I wasn't criticising her,' he said shortly. 'I just have to find her. Where is this place?'

Laura closed her eyes, thinking.

'Somewhere near a place called Moloti Pass,' she said. 'I think the convalescent home is called Thornton House, but I'm not certain. And I can't say for sure that Penny has actually gone there.'

'We'll follow that up. Thanks, Sister Kent,' he said, once again writing.

At the door, Laura turned, but he didn't look up.

She had had no thought of Penny being a possible contact, but now that this had been mentioned, she found it difficult to control her growing concern for her friend. More than once that day she had to tell herself severely that there was no real reason to worry about Penny, no real reason for this heavy apprehension she couldn't seem to shake off.

And so, in a way, she wasn't really surprised when David Mackay sent for her again.

This time he was standing at the window, and he turned round when she went in. The remote professional coolness had gone from his eyes.

'I understand you and Sister Harding are close friends?' he said unexpectedly.

Laura, her throat suddenly tight, could do nothing but nod.

'You were right about where she'd gone,' he said quietly. 'We traced her without too much trouble. The police have been very helpful.'

He drew out a chair, and Laura found she was glad to sit down.

'Two days ago,' he said, his voice even, 'Penny Harding told her friend she thought she was getting flu'. Yesterday her friend arranged for her to go into one of the private rooms at Thornton House. 'Today—' he paused, and Laura saw the lines of weariness deepen on his lean face. 'Today the Matron was on the point of phoning Durban to have her transferred there, as she felt there was something more than 'flu wrong. Fortunately, that was when we got in touch with them.'

Laura's thoughts whirled. Penny, obviously seriously ill, and a small convalescent hospital where she had been for a few days without anyone knowing that she was in the early stages of a haemorrhagic and highly infectious fever!

'What are you going to do?' she asked the doctor, not quite steadily.

He showed her a large-scale map open on the desk.

'Thornton House is there, in this small valley,' he told her.

'There's only one way in, fortunately. And, equally fortunately, there are very few patients there at the moment, and none have left in the last week. What we're going to do is this. We're going to isolate Thornton House completely. There's a police barricade there now, at the entrance to the valley, and we're going to send a team in by helicopter, a team who will stay there and deal with Sister Harding's case, and—any further cases.'

He took the map back from her.

'I'll be leading the team,' he said quietly. 'The situation here at St Luke's is in hand, and I've arranged for Dr Marsh, one of my colleagues, to fly down here. Potentially, the situation at the hospital in the hills is considerably more dangerous. I'll need a good and experienced medical team with me, Sister Kent.'

Laura looked at him, not understanding, still shaken at the thought of Penny so seriously ill.

'Sister Kent,' said David Mackay, his voice steady, his eyes holding hers, 'I'm asking you to come with me, to be part of my team.'

CHAPTER FOUR

DAVID Mackay's dark eyes were on her face, questioning now, and Laura knew she had to give him an answer.

'I'm sorry, Dr Mackay,' she began, trying to recover from her surprise that he wanted her for this special team. 'I—'

He stood up.

'I understand, Sister Kent,' he said formally, but there was disappointment in his voice. 'I know it's a lot to be asking of you, and I do understand your refusal.'

Laura stood up too.

'I'm not refusing, Dr Mackay,' she told him steadily. 'But you took me by surprise. I wasn't expecting you to want me to be part of the team, so I do need to think about it.'

Immediately, disarmingly, he smiled, and the dark eyes looking down at her were warm.

'I can give you all of five minutes to do that, Laura,' he told her, and the unexpectedness of his departure from professional formality brought a tide of colour to her cheeks.

'Let me spell it out,' he went on. 'It's dangerous— difficult—demanding. I can't be making any promises about how long we'll be there, and we'll have to make the best of medical conditions there. So—think about it, Laura, but I'm afraid you'll have to think quickly, because we leave tomorrow, and if your answer is no, I'll need to be looking for someone else.'

He sat down at his desk and began to write. Laura turned to the window and looked out, unseeing.

She knew all the things he had said, knew them and accepted them. She could handle any of them, even the very real danger of working with patients who had a highly infectious disease. The situation would, she knew, be extremely tense in this hospital in the hills. Hospital? Nothing more, really, than a small private nursing home. There was no doubt that David Mackay would need all the help he could get.

And there was Penny, her dear friend, there and in need of help.

She swung round.

'I'll come, Dr Mackay,' she said quietly.

He stood up, strode across to her and took both her hands in his.

'That's grand, lass,' he said, and the warm and real sincerity of his voice took her aback, so that it was a moment or two before she recovered, and drew her hands away from his.

'You did say we leave tomorrow?' she asked him, and he nodded.

'Lists of equipment and medical supplies are here,' he said, turning back to the big desk. 'I'd like you to read over the lists, make any suggestions you want to, and I'll want you to check supplies as they're ready. We'll be flying to Durban tomorrow—the Air Force has laid on transport for us—and from there we'll go by helicopter to the Drakensberg. Any further supplies we need will be flown in to us by helicopter, but contact will be kept to a minimum. Once we're in, the Army will seal off the valley.'

Laura nodded, accepting the gravity of the situation, and she saw approval in his eyes. She glanced at the list.

'We're taking a standard respirator?' she asked him. 'Not a transit one?'

David Mackay's dark eyes were compassionate.

'They'll be no question of transferring patients, Sister,' he told her. 'No matter how ill your friend is, or any other patient, the isolation must be complete. But our team, you and I and the others, can do as much for them as anyone in the whole country. Remember that.'

I will remember, Laura thought, and she knew that no matter what her personal feelings were for this man, her respect for him as a doctor was very high indeed. And that, she told herself, is the only thing that matters, in this situation.

David Mackay walked to the door with her.

'Dr Sheldon is to be joining Dr Marsh here,' he told her. 'He's probably here already, so you'll at least have the chance to say goodbye to him.'

There was nothing in the dark eyes looking down at her to make her feel uncomfortable, nothing in his voice to justify the warm rush of colour to her cheeks— only the memory of herself in Jeff Sheldon's arms, and David Mackay standing at the door, cool, remote. And the memory, too, of his raised eyebrows when she insisted that she and Jeff were not engaged.

'Thank you, Dr Mackay,' she said stiffly, annoyed with herself, and even more annoyed with this man who somehow managed to make her feel uncomfortable. She lifted her chin and looked at him steadily, and coolly, she hoped. 'I'll be glad to do that. Dr Sheldon and I have been friends for a long time.'

Now there was no doubt about the amusement in the big Scottish doctor's eyes.

'So I gathered, Sister Kent,' he drawled. 'So I gathered.'

And then he was professional and businesslike again, handing her a list of instructions and times, and reminding her that he would like her to be on hand to check supplies as they were loaded.

When they parted, Laura walked briskly along the corridor, glad to cool down her warm cheeks. Outside the doctors' rest room, she hesitated. Jeff might be there—she should, she knew, take the chance to see him now, if possible, before she got too busy with the preparations for leaving. Yet, remembering the way he had looked at her, the way he had held her, she was reluctant, now, to see him.

While she was trying to decide whether to knock, or to turn and go on, Jeff himself came along the corridor, smiling as he saw her.

'Told you I'd be over to join you soon,' he said cheerfully. 'Where's the Big White Chief? I'm supposed to see him before he gets himself too involved in his preparations for leaving. Never mind, between us you and I will keep things running smoothly here. Not to mention Dr Marsh, who I gather is another Big White Chief!'

Laura couldn't respond to his smile, knowing what she had to tell him.

'Jeff—' she began, hesitating, trying to choose her words.

He took both her hands in his.

'I'm sorry, love,' he said quietly. 'You must be worried about Penny, and not in the mood for any jokes. They'll do their best for her, you know that, don't you?'

Laura nodded.

'Yes, I do know that,' she replied. And then, quickly, 'Jeff, I'm going too. Dr Mackay has asked me to be part of the team.'

Now there was no laughter on his face. His hands tightened on hers.

'I don't want you to go, Laura,' he said quietly.

'I can be a useful part of the team, Jeff,' Laura pointed out, shaken by the unusual seriousness of his face. 'The experience I've had here—'

'I know that,' he interrupted her, and she knew that it was his concern that was making him brusque, impatient. 'But Laura—here at least, you're in hospital conditions, here there's a better chance of control.' He looked down at her, unsmiling. 'He had no right to ask you. I don't want you to go, Laura.'

Neither of them had heard David Mackay come along the corridor, and when he spoke, they both swung round.

'I'm sorry you feel like that, Dr Sheldon,' he said levelly. 'But Sister Kent knows what the position is. The decision, surely, is hers.'

Both doctors turned, then, to Laura.

'Laura?' said Jeff urgently.

David Mackay said nothing.

'I said I'd go,' Laura told both of them, her head held high, 'and I'm sticking to that.'

And she turned, then, and walked away, without giving either of them a chance to reply. Fond as she was of Jeff, she was annoyed at him now, for putting her in a false position, for behaving as if he had any right to tell her what to do. Dr Mackay, she thought with some reluctance, was right: the decision was hers, and no one else's.

The rest of the day flew past in a blur of activity, as the medical team prepared for an indefinite stay in the small nursing hom, cut off from the rest of the world— and dealing with a virulent and almost unknown disease. It was only late at night that Laura even had the chance to phone her mother and tell her what was happening.

When she had finished speaking, there was no reply from her mother.

'I couldn't refuse to go, Mum,' Laura said after a while, quietly.

'I know that, Laura,' her mother replied. Laura could hear, then, that she was trying to smile. 'I'd have felt the same, in my nursing days, and in theory I agree completely. Of course you must go. But nurses don't make the most relaxed mothers, love, and there's such a lot in the papers about the whole thing. I suppose they're blowing it up for the sake of news?'

'I suppose so,' Laura returned carefully. But she knew that she hadn't deceived her mother, and now she gave up the attempt. 'Mum, do something for me— ring Penny's folks. They're trying not to alarm them, obviously, but when they were trying to find out where Penny might have gone, they had to get in touch with them. I know you've only met them a couple of times, when they came down for Penny's twenty-first, but— look, you'll have to play it by ear, find out how much they know, and take it from there. I just feel they could use a friendly word. And at least you'll be able to tell them I'll be with Penny.'

'I'll do that,' her mother agreed, with a forced brightness that made Laura's heart ache.

'Give my love to Tim and Johnny,' she said quickly. 'Tell them they can use my tapes while I'm away, but no fighting about them. And Mum—Johnny can use my car to go up and down to university, it will save you some running around. He'll have to collect it from the hospital—Dad has a spare key. Give him my love too, of course.'

It was a strange feeling, she thought fleetingly, talking about her brothers, thinking about her folks, and not knowing how soon she would be at home with them. For a short time—a short time, she told herself firmly—she would be moving into a different world, a world shut off from all that was familiar.

'And give my love to Sam,' she said. 'Tell him we're going to start these training sessions as soon as I get home.'

Her mother laughed, and Laura was glad she had mentioned their large and exuberant dog.

'I'll tell him, but you can bet he won't be doing any homework. Tell me, love, what's he like, this doctor who's been brought here to take charge? Dr Mackay, isn't it? Does he know what he's doing?'

'Oh yes,' Laura replied, with no hesitation. 'He's good, Mum, he knows his stuff. Pretty sure of himself, mind, and I personally find him more than a little abrasive, but—well, he's good at his job, and that's all that really matters.'

'Looks quite nice, I thought from a couple of the newspaper photos,' her mother commented. 'Nice smile.'

'I suppose so,' Laura agreed, and unbidden and surprisingly disturbing, there was the memory of that moment in the garden when his hand had covered hers, and his face had been so close to hers. 'I gather,' she said quickly, 'he's left a trail of broken hearts behind him in Johannesburg.' And then, honesty taking over, 'Well, one, anyway. Mum, give Dad and the boys my love, I'll write. I must go now.'

'Goodbye, love,' said her mother, very steadily. 'You'll be busy, I know, but write when you can, and—take care.'

Slowly Laura replaced the receiver. Take care. Not too easy, that, with a disease that could spread as swiftly and as virulently as this one could. And there was so little certainty about the treatment for it.

For the first time in her years of nursing, she couldn't help a moment of concern for herself. After all, Penny had got it, and she had only been doing her job, just as Laura herself would be doing.

Perhaps, she thought soberly, it's just as well to be realistic about the chances we're all taking. And at least, if any one of us does come down with it, David Mackay knows as much as anyone. Because whatever I feel about him as a man, I have nothing but respect for him as a doctor, and that's all that really matters.

Before they left for the airport the following morning, she had one brief moment with Jeff, and she was glad of that, for he came over to her as she was checking the loading of their equipment and said quietly that he wanted to apologise.

'I had no right to speak to you as I did, and I'm sorry,' he told her. 'Can we forget it, and go back to where we were?'

'Of course,' Laura replied, not entirely truthfully, but she was glad to part from Jeff on good terms rather than on bad.

'I won't risk either your displeasure or Dr Mackay's by kissing you goodbye,' Jeff said, and there was a little of his old jauntiness back in his voice. 'But I'll be waiting for you when you get back, Laura.'

He left her then, walking back briskly, his white coat flying. I'm being like Scarlett O'Hara, Laura thought, ashamed of her own relief at being able to dismiss Jeff from her thoughts—I'll think about it tomorrow!

In other circumstances she would have enjoyed the helicopter flight from Durban to the small landing strip of Moloti Pass, with the breathtaking views of the sweeping Drakensberg mountains rising sheer and jagged into the clouds. But all her thoughts were on what they would find when they reached Thornton House—when she saw Penny.

Two Land Rovers were waiting to take as much as possible to the small nursing home, and they were to return until everything had been taken, and then again later, when the helicopter made another journey from Durban with the rest of the medical supplies.

'Look,' said David Mackay, as the Land Rover they were in drew away from the airstrip, and he pointed farther along the valley, to where the road wound between a grove of poplars. Laura, following his pointing finger, saw that already the road leading into and out of the valley was blocked, with large barrels right across it.

And in spite of herself she shivered, for now it was very real, that they were here in this valley, with virtually all contact with the outside world cut off.

Thornton House was little more than a large farmhouse, Laura realised, as they drew up outside it. She tried to remember what her friend Irene had said about it in her letters. Very small, and concentrating on only a few patients, who really needed little more than a pleasant place to convalesce, with a trained nursing staff in attendance if necessary.

There was a small group of people waiting at the door, and as soon as Laura jumped down from the Land Rover, Irene hurried over to meet her.

'Laura, I didn't dare to hope you might be one of the team,' she said unsteadily, and Laura's heart turned over, for redheaded Irene's usually bright, smiling face was white and anxious.

'Penny?' she asked.

Her friend hesitated, but only for a moment.

'Not too great,' she said quietly.

'Sister Kent, would you come with me? I'd like to do some planning before we set things up,' David Mackay said.

Laura hurried over to him.

'I'm sorry, Doctor,' she said quickly, annoyed at herself for once more being in the wrong with this man.

Unexpectedly, the lines of his lean brown face relaxed. Not quite a smile, she thought, but almost.

'It's all right, Sister,' he said, less formally. 'Your friend must be very glad to see you here, I'm sure.'

Laura and Jill, the other Sister, went with the doctor and Miss Durham, the Matron, through the small nursing home, and Laura, already knowing the big dark doctor, could see that he was trying to hide his dismay at the problems they were going to have to tackle.

'What we need, Miss Durham,' he said politely, 'is a room where we can set up effective isolation, where we're able to nurse any patient with effective barrier nursing. The rooms are small—we'd need a respirator in here—'

He looked around, frowning. Laura walked further along the passage and looked into a large sitting-room, with an enclosed veranda beyond it.

'Dr Mackay,' she said, hurrying back to him, 'would it not be possible for us to use these two rooms? See, we can shut off this end of the corridor almost completely, and there's a bathroom here, and enough electrical points for any of our equipment—'

The doctor strode on ahead of her, looking around him as he went, assessing, and in a moment he nodded.

'Good thought,' he said to her. 'It isn't ideal, but it's certainly the best we can do. We'll have the equipment

sent in, and I'd like you to go ahead and plan your isolation room. I'll be in and out, and if I don't agree with
you I'll tell you.'

A moment later Laura was left on her own, looking
a little helplessly at   furniture in both rooms. But
before she could do any more than try to visualise the
rooms empty, David Mackay was back, with two
young black men.

'Joseph and Henry,' he told her briefly. 'Joseph looks
after the garden here, and Henry is one of the drivers.
They'll help you to move furniture. Be ruthless—if you
want everything out, have it taken out.' At the door,
he turned. 'Oh, I'm sending your friend to help you,
Matron says it's all right.' He hesitated, then said quietly, 'As soon as we have the protective clothing
unpacked, I'll go in to see Penny. Once I've seen how
she is, we'll decide about moving her in here. Until
then, obviously contact with her is to be kept to a minimum. One of the first things we'll do is run tests on all
the people who've been in contact with her here. And
that could well be everyone.'

When he had gone, Laura, with the help of the two
men, began to get the room cleared. There were only
a few wicker chairs in the sun-room, and the two young
nurses carried them outside. Sooner than Laura had
expected, the rooms were empty, and Laura and Irene,
who had come through soon after David Mackay left,
stood surveying the space.

'It makes most sense,' Laura said slowly, 'if we use
the sun-room as the actual isolated ward. It could, at
a push, take two beds.'

At the moment, she arranged for one bed to be carried in, and the respirator placed beside it. But even
when she had set up a trolley, and made the place look
as professional as possible, it was still far from being

what she would want—and what David Mackay would want—of a hospital room. And an isolation room at that.

She said as much to Irene, and the other girl nodded.

'Miss Durham has actually tried pretty hard to get away from a hospital atmosphere,' she explained ruefully. 'Very often people coming here have had a fair spell in hospital, and they're looking for something much less formal.'

'Nice idea, unless something like this crops up,' Laura replied. So far, apart from their first few words, they had avoided talking about Penny, but now, as they waited for the next packing-case to be brought in, Laura turned to her friend.

'When did you last see Penny?' she asked.

'Yesterday morning,' Irene replied. 'Since we knew it was a haemorrhagic fever, Miss Durham hasn't allowed anyone other than herself to go in and look after Penny.'

And by that time, Laura thought bleakly, a great deal of damage could have been done, as far as contacts go.

'I know,' Irene said soberly. 'Too late by then—but it still made sense to cut down contact. Your Dr Mackay is doing the same.'

'He isn't my Dr Mackay,' Laura returned.

'Sister Kent, you've done wonders,' a familiar voice said from behind her, and she hoped she only imagined the faint hint of amusement in it. 'I came to tell you there's a protective suit ready for you, if you want to come in with me. No, I haven't seen her yet—I knew you'd be anxious.'

Already the overall, and the plastic helmet, and the boots and gloves, were so familiar to Laura that she forgot to think of how they would look to Penny, until they were actually in the room. And then, seeing her friend's fair head on the pillow, seeing, shocked, the grey pallor of her face, she wondered if Penny would even know her.

David Mackay was bending over the bed.

'Hello, Penny,' he said easily, and even though the mask Laura was conscious of the reassurance in his voice. 'Sorry about this—we'll have you feeling better soon.'

His plastic-gloved hand beckoned to Laura, and she came forward.

'I've brought a friend of yours here to help to look after you,' he said.

'Penny, it's me—Laura. How do you feel?'

'Pretty awful.' Penny's voice was only a thread, but as she looked up, she tried to smile. 'Hey, what's with the Space Odyssey business? I didn't realise I was that bad!'

And then, the effort obviously too much for her, she closed her eyes.

Behind her mask, Laura felt her own eyes fill. Dr Mackay was looking at her, and even through his mask she could see the compassion and the sympathy on his face.

And I don't want that, she thought, unnerved.

I want nothing from him at all but a professional relationship.

CHAPTER FIVE

THE girl in the bed had fallen asleep. But it was a shallow, distressed sleep, and Laura knew, looking at her friend and listening to her, that the respirator would be needed very soon, unless there was a dramatic improvement in Penny's condition. And there was nothing in their experience at St Luke's to give her any reason to hope for that.

'Thank you, Miss Durham,' David Mackay said to the Matron, who had been looking after Penny. Laura, listening to the muffled sound of his voice, through his mask and her own, had a swift, momentarily chilling foresight of the many times to come when she would stand listening to this distortion of a normal voice, as they did what they could to care for the people in the grip of this unknown and terrifying virus. You're being fanciful, she told herself severely, and this is no time or place for that. And she forced herself to push away the thoughts and to listen to David Mackay talking to Miss Durham.

'We'll be moving her just as soon as we have an isolation room set up. I know you can't be with her all the time, in fact I need to consult you, and so does my staff. Until we can get her moved, I'll have her checked regularly.'

He nodded to Laura, and she followed him out of the room. When their protective masks were off, he began to discuss their arrangements for setting up an isolation room which would have to be an intensive care room as well. Laura told him what she had managed to do so far, and free of their robes and boots as well, they went along the corridor to check on what had been the sunroom, changed now into as efficient as isolation room as Laura had been able to achieve.

David Mackay was professional and detached, and she was grateful for that, as she found it easier to deal with him on this basis.

'Thanks, Sister Kent, you've done a good job,' he said when they had finished. 'There are some tests I want to run on Penny, and on all her contacts, but Sister Derry can help me. I'd like you to spend some time with Miss Durham, and find out what you can about the other patients here. I've asked that each one should be kept in his or her room, but beyond that we're just not going to be able to do all I'd like to in the way of isolation. In any case—'

For a moment, his professional detachment was gone, and his dark eyes were bleak. In any case, isolation now could well be too late, Laura finished the thought for him.

For a moment, as their eyes met, all distance between them had gone, and they were two people with a shared concern for a difficult, perhaps impossible job.

'I'm glad you came, Laura,' David Mackay said quietly, and the complete unexpectedness of his words, together with the warmth in his dark eyes, threw her, so that she could only look at him, the colour rising in her cheeks, for a moment or two, before she murmured something—she wasn't sure what—and turned away.

He didn't mean anything personal, she told herself sensibly, as she stood outside the Matron's office. Other than that the experience I've already had is useful here.

Miss Durham was not a young woman, and Laura felt sorry for her, suddenly thrown into this crisis in her peaceful mountain nursing home. She remembered letters from Irene telling them about this nursing friend of her mother's, who had used a small inheritance to invest in the one-time guesthouse here.

'Oh, does Dr Mackay want me?' queried Miss Durham, rising to her feet.

'No, Dr Mackay is busy at the moment,' Laura told her. 'And everything is going nicely, we should be moving Penny into isolation soon.'

She told the older woman that Dr Mackay wanted her to find out about the other patients, and Miss Durham, obviously glad to be able to help, took her along the corridor to the wing where the patients had their rooms.

'Fortunately,' she said, 'we're very quiet at the moment. And no one has left since Penny got here, so there are no outside contacts to check, and she didn't go away from here at all in the few days.'

At the end of the corridor, she stopped.

'All the rooms have their own bathrooms, so it isn't too difficult to do as Dr Mackay wants, and keep the patients apart.' She stopped, as there was a loud and insistent buzz, with a red light showing above one of the doors. Irene came hurrying along, stopping as she reached them.

'It's Mr Wood, Miss Durham,' she said breathlessly. 'He's very angry at being kept in his room, and he's speaking about getting in touch with his lawyer.'

Miss Durham drew herself up, and for a moment Laura's and Irene's eyes met. Once a Matron, always a Matron, Laura thought, even in a small nursing home in the mountains.

'Thank you, nurse, you may go. I shall talk to Mr Wood myself,' said Miss Durham, and she knocked on the door and sailed in majestically, Laura following in her wake.

The man in the room was fully dressed, and his face was flushed with anger.

'Now look here, Miss Durham, this is ridiculous!' he began. 'You know very well I'm due to leave here tomorrow, and now I'm told that not only can I not leave, but I'm not allowed to go out of my room. What sort of nonsense is this?'

'I've already explained to you, Mr Wood,' the Matron replied coolly. 'You know what the position is. We have a young nurse here with a highly infectious virus, and as she was here for some time before this was discovered, all contacts must be kept under careful supervision.'

'But I hardly saw the girl!' the man protested furiously. 'For heaven's sake, Miss Durham, I'm here for nothing more than a few days' rest after having my appendix out! I have a business to run, and I've been away from it long enough. I'd like you to tell this Dr Mackay or whoever he is that I'll be leaving tomorrow. I'll give him my address in Durban if necessary.'

Laura didn't want to interfere, but she could see that the older woman was at a loss, so she stepped forward.

'Mr Wood,' she said quietly, 'I don't think you understand the position. There's already been one death at St Luke's in Cape Town, and there could be more. We're dealing with a virus we just don't know enough about, and we can't take any risks. For your own sake, please give us your co-operation.'

Slowly the angry red faded from the man's face.

'All the more reason to get away from here, then,' he muttered. 'No sense, surely, in exposing people like me to any more chance of getting this thing. Look, I'd like to speak to this doctor. Get him along here now, please.'

Laura took a deep breath.

'Dr Mackay is busy right now, but I'll give him your message,' she said, and hoped the iciness in her voice wasn't lost on him. She and the Matron went out together, closing the door behind them.

In the corridor, they looked at each other.

'Fortunately, they're not all like that,' the older woman said, and managed to smile.

The girl in the next room was young, in her early twenties. She was sitting in a chair at the window, knitting, and when they went in she turned round, smiling. Laura's heart sank as she saw that the brown-haired girl was pregnant.

'This is Mrs Benson, Sister Kent,' said the Matron, returning the girl's smile. 'Sally, Sister Kent is one of the team from Cape Town.'

Sally Benson's blue eyes met Laura's.

'All very dramatic, Sister,' she remarked. 'I've been watching all the comings and goings. How is Penny?'

The medical team had decided, in a conference on the plane, that while there was a need to keep people informed, it would serve no purpose to spread unnecessary alarm. So Laura said carefully that Penny was certainly very ill, but now they were here they hoped to see an improvement. She asked then when Sally's baby was due.

'Not for another month,' Sally told her. 'It seems like I've been pregnant for ever, because I've had to take things easy right from the start. That's why I'm here, to make me behave myself, isn't it, Matron?' For a moment, the blue eyes clouded. 'I've lost two babies before this, so I'm more than prepared to do what I'm told. But I only have to stay another week, then I'm going home, to be near the hospital. I—I just can't believe everything is still all right, after the other times.' For a moment, her hand touched the bulge under her loose dress, protectively. 'Boy or girl, this is one very active baby, though! '

They left her, then, and went on to the next room, Laura making a mental note to suggest to David Mackay that they request an incubator to be brought to them. Just in case.

The patient in the next room, Mrs Turner, was listening to the Over-Sixties Club on the radio, but she switched it off when they went in, and turned eagerly towards them.

'Oh,' she said, seeing Laura, obviously disappointed, 'I thought it would be that nice-looking doctor with the lovely Scottish voice.' Guilty colour flooded her paper-fragile face. 'It was very naughty of me, Miss Durham, but I did just creep to the end of the corridor to see what was going on, and I heard him. Such a lovely voice! My husband was Scottish, you know.'

Matron's eyes met Laura's.

'Mrs Turner,' she said firmly, 'you know very well that I told you you have to stay in your room. Until Dr Mackay decides what is to be done, we can't take any chances. So please stay in here.'

The old lady looked at Laura, obviously hoping for more sympathy.

'It's so lonely,' she sighed.

Laura hardened her heart.

'I'm sure it is, Mrs Turner,' she said, meaning it. 'But you really must do as you're told, and stay in your room. I'll tell you what—you stay right here, and perhaps later today, or tomorrow, Dr Mackay will come along and see you.'

The old lady's face brightened.

'That will be nice, dear, I'll look forward to that.' And then, remembering, 'How is that young nurse— Irene's friend? Such a friendly girl! She was in to see me quite a few times, and I was so sorry to hear how ill she is. And it must be bad, to bring you and the doctor all the way from Cape Town.'

Not to mention the rest of the team, and all the equipment, and the drugs here, and the rest on the way from America, Laura thought.

'Yes,' she said quietly, 'it is quite serious, Mrs Turner. So you see how much we need your help in doing what we ask.'

Outside the room, she turned to Miss Durham.

'There seems to have been a fair bit of contact between Penny and Mrs Turner,' she observed.

The older woman sighed.

'I know, and I've already mentioned it to Dr Mackay. Obviously, now, I wish Penny had kept to herself, but—well, there was no reason for me to keep her away from the people here. None of them are really ill, and they did enjoy new company. And she's such a friendly girl. You know Penny.'

Oh yes, Laura thought bleakly, I know Penny. Friendly, interested in people, a nurse to the last inch of her. She'd be getting to know all these people, talking to them, listening to them. Until she began to feel ill. . .

'And your last patient, Miss Durham?' she asked.

There was no imagining the cloud on Matron's face.

'He's my nephew,' she said quietly. 'My sister's son, Pieter van Heerden. He has leukaemia. He's in remis-

sion at the moment, but of course there's no telling how
long it will last. It seemed a good idea for him to have
a week or two here before he needs another course of
chemotherapy.'

She opened the door, and Laura saw the young man
on the bed was asleep with a rug thrown over him.

'No need to disturb him, Miss Durham,' she said
softly. 'I can talk to him later.'

She closed the door, but when she turned round, the
Matron was still looking at her. Laura waited.

'He and Irene have known each other all their lives,'
the older woman told her. 'You know Irene's mother
and I nursed together? Well, through the years we've
often spent holidays together, and Pieter and Irene
have always been friends.' She shook her head. 'More
than friends, in the last few years.'

Laura felt her breath catch in her throat. A vivid
memory stabbed her, a memory of their early nursing
days, and a group of them sitting in a bedroom drinking cocoa, their studying momentarily set aside. And
Irene, her red-gold curls shining as she told them about
Pieter.

'I suppose you could call him the boy back home,'
she had said, laughing, 'although he doesn't really live
near the farm. But I've known him all my life, and
he's—kind of special. We're very sensible, though—no,
really we are. I'm going to have a whale of a time here
in Cape Town, and he's going to have a whale of a time
in Johannesburg, and maybe when we've both done
that, we'll decide we still do like each other better than
all these whales!'

Miss Durham's eyes were on her face.

'You know about him,' she said sadly. 'I thought it
might help them both, bringing him here, but it doesn't

seem to have helped at all, in fact it's made things worse.'

There was nothing Laura could say, but she put her hand on the older woman's arm, just for a moment, and there was gratitude on the Matron's face before she turned away, saying briskly that she had better get back to work.

Laura followed her, and she thought now she understood the shadow in Irene's eyes. Not only anxiety for Penny, but heartbreak for herself. Perhaps there would be a chance to talk to her, later in the day, Laura thought.

But the rest of the day flew past. David Mackay wanted Penny moved to the isolation room, and when that was done, and Penny made as comfortable as possible, he and Laura and Jill Derry, the other Sister, had a brief conference to work out nursing rotas, and a tightening-up on isolation and nursing procedure for the other patients. Laura asked if she could do the first shift, and by afternoon she was installed in the room where Penny was to be nursed.

It was dusk when David Mackay came in.

'Any response to the new medication?' he asked her, his voice low. Penny had not stirred all the time Laura was with her, but that didn't mean that she couldn't hear, and Laura kept her own voice as low.

'Nothing positive yet,' she said carefully. 'But there are no signs of drug sensitivity either.'

'So we'll keep on with it,' David Mackay confirmed. He looked at the girl on the bed again. 'Poor lass,' he murmured, 'and her just doing her job. Leave her for a moment, Sister, and come next door.'

It was a relief to take the protective helmet off, even for a short time, as they went over Penny's chart together.

'She's holding her own,' the doctor said at last. 'No need for the respirator yet. Perhaps the American vaccine will do more for her, since we were able to give it to her at an earlier stage.'

More than it did for Elize Marais at St Luke's, Laura thought. It will have to do more, because it didn't save her life.

But she mustn't have thoughts like that, she told herself when David Mackay had gone, and she was back in the silent room, with Penny lying so still in the bed. She rose and sponged Penny again, deliberately keeping herself as busy and as professional as possible, trying to keep at bay the thought that this was Penny, one of her dearest friends, lying here.

When Jill Derry came in to take over, Laura knew she should go right to bed, for she was exhausted. But she was almost too tired to sleep, and she knew the feeling well enough to change into a track suit and go to the small kitchen made available to them for anything they needed through the night. She made herself a cup of hot chocolate, and tried to remember where the small sitting-room with the fire was. Perhaps if she sat down at the fire for ten minutes, while she had her hot drink, she'd be able to sleep after that.

There was a silence and a stillness that you never found in a hospital in the middle of the night, she thought. Not that it was so late, but everyone else seemed to have gone to bed. There were only dim lights in the corridor. Was this the small sitting-room? She pushed the door, tentatively, and looked into the room lit only by the glow of the fire. It was only when she sat down on the rug beside the fire that she saw David Mackay sitting on the couch.

'Oh—I'm sorry, Dr Mackay, I didn't see you!' she exclaimed, taken aback.

'We must have just missed each other in the kitchen, Sister Kent,' the doctor said, and he indicated his own steaming mug. 'Mine's coffee, what's yours? Chocolate? That should help you to sleep—mine is to keep me awake.'

She looked at him.

'You think something is going to happen with Penny,' she said flatly.

In the dim glow of the firelight, she felt his eyes on her.

'You have an uncanny knack, Sister Kent, of reading my mind,' he replied. 'Look, I have absolutely nothing to go on, just a gut feeling. You know that feeling?'

Laura nodded.

'In that case, I'll stick around too,' she said.

He shook his head.

'No, Laura,' he said firmly, 'I won't let you do that. You must have some sleep—I've had a couple of hours. And if I'm right, you'll need to be rested to take over. Because it's harder, isn't it, nursing someone who's close to you?'

Again she nodded, all at once unable to speak for a little while.

'I haven't done it before,' she said at last. 'It isn't easy, keeping a professional detachment.'

'No, it isn't easy,' David Mackay agreed, his voice warm. 'You're doing fine. Do you think you can keep it up?'

'I think so,' said Laura, and to her horror her voice was a little unsteady. 'I hadn't realised it would be so hard.'

There was a movement beside her, and David Mackay was sitting close to her, in front of the fire. He took the mug of chocolate from her hands.

'Let yourelf have a wee cry if you want to, Laura,' he said, softly. 'You'll feel better.'

Afterwards Laura, bewildered, couldn't understand how it could have happened. But suddenly there was no holding back the tears, they were running down her face, and David Mackay's arms were around her, holding her close to him, her tears soaking into the shoulder of his thick jersey. And then, when the tears were at last over, he took out his handkerchief and dried her eyes, a little clumsily, a little awkwardly.

'There, Laura, there, lass,' he soothed.

In the firelight, he was very close to her. His hand smoothed the soft red hair back from her forehead, then brushed her cheek and touched her lips lingeringly.

He drew hr towards him and his lips found hers, in a kiss that was gentle, comforting.

And then suddenly, not at all gentle, but urgent, demanding.

CHAPTER SIX

DAVID Mackay looked down at her in the dim glow
of the fire and smiled.

'I should be saying I'm sorry, Laura,' he said to her,
softly. 'But I couldn't be saying that, for it would be a
lie. At the same time, though, I didn't mean this to
happen. Not yet.'

Not yet?

'It was just a natural reaction,' Laura said hurriedly,
trying to regain some composure. 'I didn't mean to cry.
I suppose it was a safety valve, I was more upset about
Penny than I was admitting to myself, and you were
there, and you were kind and sympathetic, and—'

Even in the firelight, there was no mistaking the
amusement in his dark eyes.

'Yes? Go on, Laura, this is interesting. I don't know
I've ever had a kiss dissected scientifically before,' he
said drily.

Laura felt warm colour flood her cheeks.

'That's all, really,' she said, stiffly now. But she hesitated, disturbed by the words he had used. Not yet, he
had said. As if—

'Dr Mackay—' she began, with difficulty.

The big doctor laughed softly.

'Now, Laura,' he said reproachfully, 'surely you
can't be calling me Dr Mackay, and us just been on
kissing terms. At least, not at a moment like this. Can
you not be saying David, when we are not in a professional situation, of course?'

His voice was warm and teasing, and he was so different from her picture of him, that she was thrown, uncertain how to respond to him. But he had been kind, there was no doubt about that.

'David,' she said, troubled, 'I think—'

But before she could even try to put her thoughts into words his bleeper sounded, low and insistent. Instantly he was on his feet, pulling on the white coat that was lying on the couch, then striding along the dimly-lit corridor, towards the room where Penny lay.

Laura hurried along after him, even though she was off duty. Their protective clothing was ready, and swiftly, gowned and helmeted, they joined Jill Derry.

'Respirator,' David Mackay said curtly, and Laura brought the respirator forward, responding completely professionally to the situation. This was what they had feared, and it was severe breathing problems in the woman at St Luke's, that had signalled a rapid deterioration of her complete condition.

The three of them worked together, silently, efficiently, until Penny's condition had stabilised. Then David Mackay turned to Laura.

'Sister Kent, you'd better go off now,' he said quietly, and there was nothing in his eyes or in his voice to tell her that this was the same man who had held her in his arms in the firelight such a short time ago. And of course, Laura reminded herself quickly, that was exactly as she wanted it to be, for it was a moment best forgotten by both of them.

Through their masks, her eyes met his.

'She's all right for the moment,' he reminded her. 'There's nothing else we can do. Sister Derry will be with her. I'll stay a little longer, then I'll be on call.'

Laura, with some reluctance, went off duty, and now she was so completely drained and exhausted that she fell asleep immediately, waking hours later with winter sunshine streaming into her room, for she hadn't even pulled the curtains. There was just time for a quick bath, and something to eat, before she went to take over from Jill Derry.

She had just finished a quick cup of coffee when the dark-haired nurse brought her a message.

'Dr Mackay would like to see you before you go on duty,' she said.

Laura thanked her, and went along to the room David Mackay was using as an office. The door was a little open, and as she raised her hand to knock, she saw that the man at the desk was tired. Very tired.

And something more. She knew that immediately, from the shadow in David Mackay's eyes as he looked up at her knock, and told her to come in.

'Sit down, Sister Kent,' he said.

But for a moment Laura could do nothing but stand and look at him.

'Penny?' she said at last, not quite steadily. 'Is she worse?'

But she knew, even before he spoke, that it wasn't Penny.

'No, she's much the same, holding her own on the respirator. And I'm hoping she'll show some response to the drugs soon.' He looked down at the notes he had been working on, then he raised his head and looked at her. 'Staff Nurse Abbott—Susan Abbott—at St Luke's, the young nurse who was in intensive care when we left. She died last night. And there are two more cases, and five suspects waiting for confirmation.'

He rubbed his forehead wearily.

'I've just asked Dr Marsh to contact a fellow I worked with in Kinshasa, he's doing research in

America now. I heard from him some time ago, and I know he's working on an antidote for haemorrhagic fevers—Congo, Lassa, Marburg, and all the mutations, including the one we're dealing with now. I don't know what stage his work has reached, but if there's the slightest possibility of using that antidote, I want it. For Penny, and for all these other people.'

He looked down again at his notes.

'I thought you should know what the situation is,' he said, without looking up. 'Ask Sister Derry to come in when she comes off duty, will you?' Laura had reached the door when his voice stopped her. 'Sister Kent, some time later I want to have a talk with you about the patients here. Perhaps when I'm clear of this, one of the staff nurses can relieve you for a bit.'

It was late afternoon before he sent for Laura, and she couldn't help feeling relieved to come out of the intensive care room, away from the still figure in the bed, and the relentless, regular sound of the respirator. And yet without it, Penny wouldn't stand a chance.

'How is she?' asked David Mackay as she sat down, although just an hour ago he had looked in and checked the chart.

'No worse,' Laura told him steadily, and they both heard, all too clearly, in the silence between them, the unspoken words: And no better.

'Right, is there anything particular I should know about these people?' David Mackay said, eventually. 'I have their files. Anything beyond that?'

'Yes, I think there is,' she replied. 'It's only a precaution, but I'd feel happier if we asked for an incubator. There's no sign of Mrs Benson not going to full term, but with her history, and with things as they are here, I'd feel happier.'

The doctor scribbled a note on his pad.

'Good thinking, Sister,' he said. 'And the others? A bit fed up at being kept here, I suppose.'

'One of them in particular,' Laura told him. 'Mr Wood is talking about getting in touch with his lawyer, and he insists on seeing you. Oh, and Mrs Turner isn't giving any trouble, but I did promise her you'd look in and see her too.'

'Any special reason?' he asked. 'Is she worried about this whole situation—needing reassurance?'

'Oh, no,' she answered. 'She just wants to see the doctor with the lovely Scottish voice!'

David Mackay laughed, the lines of strain on his face disappearing.

'Well, well, it will be a pleasure to visit her.' He looked at his watch. 'I'm expecting another call from Cape Town in half an hour, when Dr Marsh has finished his rounds. Let's look in on these people now.'

Both Sally Benson and Pieter van Heerden were asleep, but Mrs Turner was sitting at her window. When they went in she looked round, her face lighting up.

'Oh, my dear, you did bring him,' she said, obviously delighted. 'Did Sister tell you that my husband was Scottish, Dr Mackay?'

David Mackay sat down on the other chair.

'No, she didn't,' he said. 'Where did he come from?'

'From Edinburgh,' she told him. 'And yourself? Is your home near there?'

He shook his head.

'No, I'm from Inverness,' he said. 'But I know Edinburgh well, that's where I went to university. You'll have been there yourself, have you?'

'No, we never had the money, but Keith talked about it so much, I feel I know it,' the old lady said softly.

David Mackay took both her hands in his.

'I have some photos that I took the last time I was in Edinburgh,' he told her. 'I'll bring them and show them to you. I'm afraid we have to go now, but that's a promise.'

Outside her door, he looked down at Laura.

'Help me to remember that, will you, Laura?' he said. 'I wouldn't want to forget.'

How strange, thought Laura, unable to stop herself, that the man who doesn't want to break a promise to an old lady, is the same man who apparently didn't mind breaking promises to that nurse. And the same man who can give a qualified Sister a bawling-out as if she was a probationer.

She lifted her chin.

'Yes, I'll remind you, Dr Mackay,' she said clearly. 'This is Mr Wood's room here.'

Harry Wood's suitcase was closed now, strapped and ready to go. He whirled round from the window when they went in, and he looked, Laura thought, even more angry than he had done yesterday.

'Dr Mackay? About time too,' he said brusquely. 'How long is this charade going to go on? I'm a busy man, and I have to get back. I'm sorry about your problems, but I have my problems too, or I will have unless I get back to Durban soon.' He took a card from his pocket. 'Now, this is my business address, and my home telephone number is there too. You can get in touch with me any time you need to. All right?'

'I'm afraid not, Mr Wood,' the big doctor said, and his voice was level. 'I don't think you quite understand the position. You're a contact—'

'Never spoke to the girl,' the other man cut in.

'All right, a possible contact, then, of a patient with a highly infectious virus, a virus that is in many ways an unknown quantity to us. For your own safety, we have to keep you here.'

Some of the colour left Harry Wood's face.

'This is the same thing the woman in Cape Town died of?' he asked. 'In that case, I say all the more reason to let people like me go. It's criminal to expose us to any more risks!'

Laura, looking at David Mackay, saw that his patience was wearing thin.

'I'm sorry, Mr Wood,' he said, his voice very cool. 'We've made the only decision possible in the circumstances, and I'm afraid you have no choice but to stay.'

The Durban businessman took a step closer.

'Look, Doctor, I haven't got where I am now without knowing there are always ways round these things.' His voice dropped. 'I'll make it well worth your while—and of course the same goes for Nurse here.'

Involuntarily, Laura's eyes flew to David Mackay's face. He was white with anger, his dark eyes narrowed, and the line of his jaw hard.

'I shall try to forget you said that, Mr Wood,' he said, very quietly, 'or you might find yourself up on a criminal charge.' He looked down at Laura, standing very still beside him. 'Sister Kent, I'm giving the order that Mr Wood's door is to be kept locked at all times. I do not intend to give any reason for this order, unless it's necessary.'

He turned on his heel, took the key from the door, waited for Laura to go out, then closed and locked the door. He was still very pale.

'Take the key to Miss Durham, would you, Sister Kent?' he said, handing it to her. 'It will be needed when his food is taken to him. Obviously, the other three people don't need to be treated in the same way.'

He strode off down the corridor, his white coat flying. And that is one angry man! Laura thought, shaken. He had, of course, every right to be angry, but she had the sudden renewed certainty that she wouldn't like to be on the receiving end of David Mackay's anger.

When she had given the key to Miss Durham—and it was interesting, Laura thought, that the older woman asked for no explanation, and didn't seem to find it strange that David Mackay had judged this necessary—she went back to the intensive care room, and Penny.

'I've just done the hourly temperature,' the dark-haired nurse, Gwen Lund, told her.

'Thanks, Nurse,' Laura replied, confirming with a glance that there was no change in Penny's temperature. 'You can go now.'

But when she had completed her own check on Penny, and made a small adjustment to the respirator, she was surprised to see that Gwen Lund was still there.

'Better take your off-duty when you can,' she said, smiling. 'We do appreciate Miss Durham allowing her staff to volunteer to help us at this end, but we don't want to take advantage of you. And if we do have any more patients, we might have to work double shifts, so grab any off duty time when you can.'

The dark-haired nurse shrugged.

'I'm not in a hurry,' she said. 'Actually, I was wondering if Dr Mackay might be coming along—he hasn't been in for a bit, he's probably due to come along soon.'

Surprised, Laura looked at the other girl.

'As far as I know, Nurse,' she said evenly, 'Dr Mackay is waiting for a call from Cape Town. He may be along here after that, but it could be some time. I doubt that it's worth your while waiting.'

Gwen Lund smiled.

'I don't know about that,' she said softly. 'Personally, I'd think a little while waiting to see Dr Mackay is well worth while. Or do you plan on keeping him all for yourself?'

Laura felt as if all the breath had been knocked from her body.

'Nurse Lund,' she said, and it wasn't easy to keep her voice steady, 'you and I are here to do a job of work, not to—to discuss Dr Mackay.'

The other girl said nothing, but there was something in her smile that made Laura, normally even-tempered, now very angry.

'And another thing,' she went on, 'in any hospital I've worked in, you don't speak to a Sister in that way.'

The dark-haired girl turned away, but when she reached the door, she glanced over her shoulder.

'That, Sister Kent,' she said sweetly, 'is precisely why I choose to work here. Miss Durham is so glad to get staff here that she runs things fairly casually. So if you're thinking of complaining to her, don't. She needs me here.'

It was only when the door had closed behind her that Laura's sense of humour reasserted itself. And what, she asked herself, would David Mackay think about a Sister and a nurse almost coming to blows about him? Silly girl, Gwen Lund, and not worth bothering about. And with that, Laura dismissed the dark-haired girl from her thoughts and concentrated on looking after Penny, monitoring every aspect of her condition, and watching for any deterioration. Once, the girl on the bed stirred, and Laura bent over her, hoping that through the plastic helmet Penny would recognise her. But her friend's eyes were dull and glazed and completely without recognition, and it was almost a relief when she closed them again.

Again, it was dark when she came off duty, and she went to the small dining-room, collected a plate of food, and put it in the microwave oven. It was only when she turned to go to the table that she saw Irene, sitting with a plate of hardly-touched food in front of her.

'Hi, Laura,' said Irene, and tried to smile. 'You folks at your end seem to be pretty busy. How's Penny?'

'Much the same,' Laura told her. 'You know she's on a respirator?'

'Yes, I know,' Irene replied, her voice low. 'Doesn't look too good, that.'

But it wasn't only concern for Penny that was causing the dark shadows under Irene's blue eyes and the droop of her red-gold head.

'Irene,' Laura said gently, 'I've just heard about Pieter. How dreadful for you. I haven't seen him yet. How is he? Miss Durham says he's in remission now—'

They both knew well enough what that meant. The period of remission could go on, or it could end, suddenly.

'He's not at all bad, at the moment,' said Irene wearily. 'That's why I want—'

She stopped, her voice all at once unsteady, and Laura waited, seeing that Irene needed to talk.

'That's why I want us to get married now,' she went on at last, her voice controlled again. 'We were talking about it, you know, before—before this happened. We hadn't got around to getting engaged or anything, but we both knew. But we thought there was no hurry, we thought we had all the time in the world. And now we don't. And Pieter doesn't think it's fair for me to marry a man who's dying!'

She was beyond tears, her face white and set. Laura put her hand over Irene's, on the table, and sat silent.

'Thanks, Laura,' her friend said at last, quietly. She drew her hand back and stood up. 'I have to go. And somehow, some time, I have to make a very stubborn man see that I'd rather have a few months with him than a lifetime with anyone else!'

She looked down.

'Come along with me and see Pieter,' she suggested. 'I'll wait until you've finished. Maybe you can make him see some sense.'

Laura couldn't hide her dismay.

'I'll come and see Pieter,' she said, after a moment. 'And of course I'll do what I can. But not right away, and certainly not at our first meeting. I couldn't do that. Let me get to know him a bit first.'

Irene's blue eyes held hers.

'Thank you, Laura,' she said, softly. 'But don't leave it too long. We don't have much time, Pieter and I.'

CHAPTER SEVEN

YOU wouldn't have known, thought Laura, looking at Pieter van Heerden, how seriously ill he was. All right, he was a little pale, perhaps thinner than she remembered him from Irene's photographs. But no more than that.

But when his grey eyes met hers, she did know. In her years of nursing she had seen too many people with that distance, that remoteness, in their eyes, not to know that they were already walking along that last, lonely road.

'Nice to meet you at last, Laura,' Pieter said. 'The only time I came to Cape Town while Irene was training, I think you were away on holiday. I'd met Penny, of course, she's come home with Irene a couple of times. Things aren't going too well with her, I hear. I've only met Dr Mackay briefly, but he seems the sort of fellow who inspires confidence, and the newspapers speak well of him. Lucky for Penny that he's here, I'd say.'

'Yes, he does inspire confidence,' Laura agreed. 'In patients and in the people who work with him.' And that was true, she thought, but it no longer surprised her to have to accept David Mackay's abilities as a doctor.

She looked again at the young man Irene loved, and thought, as she had thought before, that when it came to something like this, there were two kinds of people. One kind refused to accept the reality of their illness, and fixed their minds determinedly on one more treatment, one more operation, that would put everything right. And very often this was the best thing, for they went on fighting, and that was so important.

The other kind wanted the truth. They wanted to know everything, and to accept everything, and to come to terms with it. And if that was the right way for them, you owed it to them to give them the truth.

Which kind was Pieter van Heerden?

'How are you yourself, Pieter?' she asked, fairly cautiously. 'Your aunt told me you'd had chemotherapy—that can leave you feeling fairly miserable.'

'Yes, it did,' he replied. 'But anything is worth trying. I have some reservations about the long-term success, but I'm prepared to go along with anything they can think up. Anyway, I've got over the side effects now, and everything is all right at the moment, so I'm just taking each day as it comes, and making the most of it. Without being other than realistic.'

Irene, standing at the window, her red-gold curls shining in the sunshine, spoke without looking round.

'Are you making the most of each day, Pieter?' she asked. 'Are you really doing that?'

For a moment, Pieter van Heerden's eyes met Laura's, and the remoteness had gone.

'Yes,' he said, not quite evenly. 'Yes, I am, Irene, in the way I think best.' Then, with an effort that was all too obvious to Laura, he smiled. 'What's good enough for Frank Sinatra's good enough for me—I'll do it my way.' He stood up. 'I wish I could offer to walk you girls back, but as you know all too well, I'm confined to quarters. Come and see me again, Laura, if you have time. See you later, Irene.'

Irene turned round, her chin raised.

'I wasn't meaning to leave yet, Pieter,' she said steadily. 'I'm off duty for another hour.'

For a long time they stood looking at each other, the young man and the red-haired girl, and Laura's heart ached for both of them.

'Sorry, Irene, but I have that Criminal Law assignment to finish off and send away,' Pieter said.

For a moment, Irene looked as if she was going to say something else, then she turned and followed Laura out of the room. The two nurses walked along the corridor in silence, until at last Irene burst out,

'He goes on with his damned law degree, as if—as if he expects to have a future, but he won't let us get married! What kind of mixed-up thinking is that, Laura?'

'I don't know,' Laura said honestly. 'But maybe he has to work it out himself, Irene, maybe he just needs more time.'

Irene's clear blue eyes met hers.

'Time,' she said bleakly, 'is just what he doesn't have. Sorry, Laura—thanks for coming with me.'

Laura watched her walk down the corridor, slim and straight in her white uniform, her red head held high. I wish I could do something to help, she thought, but it's something no one else can decide for them. Maybe, though, when I know Pieter better, he'll talk to me.

She looked at her watch. Time for the daily medical conference, when David Mackay put the medical team from St. Luke's in the picture with what was happening at the big hospital, as well as discussing anything here in their hospital in the hills.

The news from Cape Town was a little better, for there was no further deterioration in the condition of the people who had developed the virus.

'But that doesn't mean to say they'll recover,' David Mackay reminded them soberly. 'The clinical picture can change very quickly—too quickly. I'm still pushing Newton in America, on his antidote, but he's reluctant to let us have it before he runs further tests. Dr Marsh is dealing with this, but I may have to come in on it, and lean on Newton some more.' He rose from the desk he had been sitting on, looked around, and smiled. 'That's all folks, and thanks. Oh, Sister Kent, wait a moment, will you?'

When the others had gone, and there were only the two of them in the room, he looked up from his notes.

'I have a message for you, Laura,' he said unexpectedly. 'I thought you would prefer to be given it on your own. It's from Dr Sheldon. He asked me to give you his love, and to tell you to look after yourself.'

Oh, Jeff! Laura thought, half amused, half angry.

'Thank you, Dr Mackay,' she replied, ignoring his use of her Christian name, for this was, after all, a professional meeting. She turned to leave.

'I could give him a message in return next time, if you want,' the doctor offered, and she wasn't sure what it was in his dark eyes as they held hers.

'Thank you, but that won't be necessary.' She hesitated. 'As I told you, Dr Sheldon and I are old friends. It amuses him to do things like this.'

It amused Dr Mackay, too, she could see, to see her somewhat at a loss.

'Of course,' he agreed. 'Old friends.' Then the amusement left his eyes and he walked across the room to where she stood, at the door. 'You're sure that's all, Laura? You're not engaged to him?'

You can't, Laura reminded herself, just say to a doctor that your private life is none of his business.

'No, I'm not engaged to Jeff Sheldon,' she said evenly.

She would have moved away, then, but his hand on her arm stopped her.

'I'm glad of that, Laura.' His voice was low. 'Very glad.'

And once again she was at a loss. For a long time, it seemed to her, they stood there, David Mackay's hand lightly on her arm. And then, not caring whether it was rude or professional, Laura turned and went out of the room, determined to put the strange little incident out of her mind entirely.

And she succeeded in that, while she was working. But when she was off duty, and out in the garden for fresh air, it kept coming back to her. He was speaking from a purely professional point of view, she told herself soberly and sensibly. If, for instance, Jeff as part of the medical team had to come here to help out, David Mackay would prefer not to have any emotional involvements between his staff. So—so of course that was why he was glad she and Jeff weren't engaged.

But there was another memory that kept coming back to her, the memory of David's lips warm and demanding on hers, and his voice, husky and not quite steady, telling her he hadn't meant this to happen. Not yet.

Laura stood up from the garden bench she had been sitting on. We're all under considerable strain, she reminded herself. It isn't really strange if we do or say things that show that tension, that's all.

Restless and troubled, in spite of that, she decided to walk briskly down to the river. That, she told herself, would be better than allowing herself to think disturbing thoughts. And perhaps tomorrow, when she had the whole morning off, she would walk up the mountainside and try to find the cave with the Bushman paintings.

She was halfway along the path down to the river when she caught a movement ahead of her, where the path turned down to a shallow ford. Someone else looking for fresh air and exercise, she thought, and she decided to turn back, because she didn't really want any company at the moment.

But something—she was never sure what—made her change her mind, and instead go to the corner of the path, where she could see the ford, and the stepping-stones.

There was a man halfway across, stepping carefully from one stone to another. We're not supposed to cross the river here, Laura thought, surprised, because it comes too near the road.

Then she saw that the man was Harry Wood. He was carrying a small hand case, and he had a jacket on with his casual slacks.

'Mr Wood!' Laura called, and ran down the path towards the river, and across the stepping-stones towards him. 'Mr Wood, what do you think you're doing? Come back!'

He turned round, and now she was close enough to see the fury on his face.

'No, thank you, Nurse,' he said grimly. 'I'm on my way, and no one is going to stop me.'

Laura was close enough to grab his arm now, but as her hand touched him he pushed her, viciously, and she fell, managing to save herself from actually falling into the water. But when she was on her feet again, Harry Wood had reached the other side and was hurrying up the path.

Laura hesitated, but only for a moment. She didn't have a chance of catching him, the only thing to do was to hurry back and get a message to the police at the road-block. She had scraped her knee on a stone in the river when she fell, but that didn't stop her running back up the path towards the big house, working out as she ran the best thing to do right away.

But as she reached the shrubbery, a tall figure in a white coat came striding round the corner, stopping in amazement as she almost hurtled into him.

'Laura, what's wrong?' demanded David Mackay.

'Harry Wood—he's got out somehow, and he's just crossed the river, he's up the other side!' she gasped, breathless.

For a moment he stared down at her.

'Stay here,' he told her decisively. 'I'll be back.'

Laura leaned against the wall, struggling to get her breath back, and she was only just breathing normally when David Mackay was back.

'Road patrol is alerted,' he told her. 'But they say that when he sees them, he might double back. Can you take me to where he crossed?'

He followed her back down the path to the river, and across to the other side. The path led up over a hill, and then down towards the road. Somewhere along the road that led from Moloti Valley and Thornton House, back towards the main road, the police from the road-block should be able to pick up Harry Wood.

'All right?' asked David, pausing halfway up the steep path to take Laura's hand and pull her up past a boulder. 'You know, if he sees them coming, he might head back this way, thinking he could make for the Pass instead.

They climbed the rest of the way to the top in silence. Laura's knee was beginning to throb where she had grazed it, and each breath hurt her throat. But she knew they could not risk letting Harry Wood escape. All right, if he did get away the police would pick him up in Durban before long. But they couldn't take the chance of letting him move freely for any length of time, because it was it was possible that he might be infected with the virus, that he might infect other people before he was caught.

'Laura, keep still!'

David Mackay's voice was low, urgent, and his hand beckoned her to draw back. He was ahead of her, looking down to where the mountain path reached the road.

'He's seen them, and he's turned back. I think he's going to head back the way the he came—it's his only chance of making for the Pass. As long as he doesn't see us, he'll think it's safe to come back this way.'

Cautiously he edged back beside her, in the shelter of a huge rock at the side of the path. Here, right in the mountains, it was so still, so quiet, that they could hear Harry Wood's laboured breathing as he climbed the path towards where they lay hidden.

And Laura, waiting, thought of the desperation on the man's face. She put her hand on the doctor's arm, and her lips close to his ear.

'Be careful—he's desperate, David!'

For a moment his hand covered hers, and he moved closer to the path, his body crouched, ready.

The laboured breathing was very close now, then she saw the man's head appear over the brow of the hill, looking back downwards. Because of that, he didn't see David, and the doctor's attack took him by surprise. The two men rolled on the mountain path, and Laura, unable to do anything to help, saw that although David had the advantage of size, and of surprise, the other man's sheer desperation counted for a great deal.

Then suddenly it was over, and David had the other man's arms pinned behind him.

'Take my tie off, Laura, and tie his hands together,' the doctor said, breathing heavily. 'Good girl, that's right.'

At the brow of the hill, two policemen appeared.

'We'll take him back for you,' one of them said.

David shook his head.

'Thanks, but I don't want him to have any contacts at all—don't come any nearer. I think we can manage him. You all right, Laura?'

'Fine,' Laura replied, not entirely truthfully, for now her grazed leg was stiffening up, and as she followed the doctor and his prisoner down the path, every step hurt, especially as she had to divide her attention between the steep path and the man who had tried so hard to escape. But soon she saw that all the fight had gone out of him, and when they reached Thornton House and took him to his room, he sat down on the chair when David untied his hands, completely finished.

His food tray lay on the floor, a plate broken, a cup of coffee spilt.

'I suppose you went for the girl who came to take your tray away—I hope she's recovered now,' the doctor said coldly. 'We'll see that you don't get another chance like that.' He glanced at Laura. 'Let's go, Sister.'

The man in the chair looked up.

'Doctor Mackay,' he said, and now there was nothing but defeat in his voice, 'I have to tell you something. I'm a businessman, and you probably won't understand this, but sometimes I have to take chances—move funds between different enterprises. Then I have to move them back again. That's why I had to get away—if I'm not able to do some sorting out, I'm in trouble. Big trouble.'

David, his hand on the door, looked back at the man, his dark eyes remote, his lean face still.

'I guess it isn't anything to do with me, and I don't think I have any right to judge the way you go about things, Mr Wood,' he said at last. 'Is there anyone who could take care of this for you—anyone you could telephone?'

Harry Wood hesitated.

'There's my partner,' he replied. 'He—doesn't actually know the full story, but he does have the authority to move funds.'

'Then I think you'd better tell him your story, and sort out your problems as far as he's concerned afterwards. I'll make arrangements for you to use my office for your phone call.'

He locked the door, ignoring the man's thanks, then he looked down at Laura.

'You look a little disapproving, Sister Kent,' he remarked. 'But I'm a doctor, not a judge of anyone's morals. I'm sorry if you disapprove.'

Laura shook her head.

'I don't,' she told him, meaning it. 'I'm just surprised.'

Surprised, she thought, at yet another example of understanding and compassion from a man I thought would be incapable of that.

He shrugged, and turned to walk along the corridor. Laura, following him, was unable to stifle a little gasp as she put her weight on the leg that had been hurt. Instantly, David swung round.

'Something wrong?' he asked her.

'Only a graze. Harry Wood pushed me, and I fell. It's nothing, really,' she protested.

'Let's have a look at it,' he said.

In the small sitting-room Laura sat down, and with considerable reluctance, rolled up the leg of her track suit.

'You're right, only a graze,' David agreed. 'But not helped any by all this rushing up and down mountain paths. Sit still—I'll clean it up for you, just to make sure.'

In spite of her protests, he was back from the kitchen in a moment, with a bowl of hot water and some cottonwool and disinfectant. His big hands were strong and confident, and yet gentle.

'I could do that myself,' Laura protested.

'I know that,' he agreed. 'There, that looks better.' He smiled, and suddenly there was something boyish and disarming about him. 'I can't think when I last attended to a grazed knee—you get a bit removed from these ordinary things, in my line!'

A little awkwardly, he rolled down the leg of her track suit, took both her hands in his, and drew her to her feet.

'I think you'll live, Sister Kent,' he said lightly.

He lifted the bowl and the disinfectant, and went out, and for some reason unknown to Laura, he was whistling.

I thought I knew him, she thought, strangely disturbed. But—I wonder, sometimes, if I really do know anything about him at all?

CHAPTER EIGHT

FROM that first moment they met, there had been this—hostility, this antagonism between them.

Laura, disturbed now by yet another unexpected side to David Mackay, reminded herself of it—reminded herself, too, of his arrogance, his high-handed ways, that first day, and the time he had come on Jeff and her in the garden.

Not to mention that nurse in Johannesburg. Oh, no, Dr David Mackay, Laura told herself, a little surface kindness from time to time doesn't change the real you, or the way I think about you. Although why I'm spending time thinking at all about a man I don't like, I don't know.

But there wasn't to be much more time for thinking, for the next day blood tests confirmed that Mrs Turner had developed the virus. David Mackay, making his daily report to the medical team, looked grave.

'She's not young, and she's not strong,' he said worriedly. 'At the moment the clinical picture is much the same as with the other cases. She has the same 'fluey symptoms—headache, shivery. We're hitting the virus with everything, but with this old lady, I'm concerned even more about side-effects. We're watching for any kidney damage, and we're watching for possible strain on her heart. I want to be informed immediately there's any change at all in her condition.'

He looked down at his notes.

'Mr Wood,' he said levelly, 'is showing a slightly raised temperature. I think you all know of his attempted escape—perhaps this is no more than a reaction to all his exertions, which came to nothing, thanks to the prompt action on the part of Sister Kent. But we're taking hourly temperatures, and we may have to bring him through here to the isolation unit too. All this, of course, puts extra pressure on all of us—we may need extra staff before long.' He looked around and smiled in dismissal, but Laura could see the weariness in his dark eyes. He had been up most of the night, she knew, for Penny had had a convulsion, and he had been called, and he hadn't been happy about her condition since then.

Laura herself was just going on duty. No matter how hard she tried to feel positive, each time she went in and saw Penny lying so still and white, she felt herself losing hope of her friend's recovery. She hadn't been on duty when Penny had had the convulsion, but Jill Derry had told her how bad it was. There was a very real danger of the same thing happening again, and so Laura was watching for the first signs of any airway obstruction. If they could deal with that before Penny had another convulsion, there would be less danger of any brain damage.

And so, the moment she saw a sustained contraction of the abdominal muscles, and then a seesaw movement of the chest, she pressed the bleeper. David was there so quickly that she realised, later, he couldn't have gone to bed.

But at that moment there was time for nothing but Penny's condition, and the need for immediate action.

'Tracheotomy, Sister Kent,' David said brusquely. 'Instruments ready?'

The instruments were sterilised ready for just such an emergency, and the tracheotomy tray was prepared. The procedure was familiar enough to Laura, the opening made in the tracheal rings, and the cuffed tube inserted. She and David worked together in silence, and his nod of approval as she handed him the right instrument, was enough commendation. He stayed with her until he was satisfied that the vital signs had stabilised, then beckoned her to the far side of the room.

'You know the post-operative care, Sister Kent,' he said, his voice low. 'I want her kept in a semi-Fowler's position to facilitate respiration and to promote draining and minimize oedema. What we have to watch is the reaction to some of the drugs she's already on—we can't take her off anything, but there's a risk of some of them depressing the cough reflex.' Over the mask his eyes met hers in a brief smile. 'We avoided another convulsion, with you calling me so promptly. Don't hesitate if you need me again.'

It was a long, long night.

Penny's condition remained stable, but there was an additional strain in checking the tubes, making certain that the trauma of the tracheotomy had not had any further effect on her. But it was only when Jill Derry came on duty that Laura realised just how exhausted she was. She went to her room and collapsed into a deep sleep, oblivious of any sounds around her, waking when the late afternoon sun was beginning to go down. She showered and pulled on her track suit, determined to get some fresh air before the day was entirely gone. But before she went out, she decided to look in on Sally Benson. She had become quite friendly with the young mother-to-be, dropping in whenever she could, as she knew that Sally, uncomplaining as she was, was lonely and very often bored.

Today her face lit up when Laura knocked and went in.

'I refuse to do any more knitting,' she said, smiling. 'This child already has far too much. I've improved, though—the first thing I knitted was little baggy trousers, and I was so pleased with them until Neil said they were lovely, but unfortunately they had two left legs, and he doubted if any child of his would have the same!'

The laughter left her face.

'I was just asking Dr Mackay about Mrs Turner,' she said. 'He was in a little while ago. He says she's very bright, in spite of not feeling too great. He'd been showing her pictures of Edinburgh, and said it was incredible what she knew about it, although she's never been there. Laura, it isn't just 'flu she's got, is it? She has this awful virus, hasn't she?'

Laura hesitated, but it was obvious that Sally didn't have many doubts. And often the truth was easier to deal with than vague fears.

'Yes, she has, Sally,' she said soberly. 'So far, she isn't too bad, but of course she's far from young, and not too strong.'

Sally's blue eyes were clouded.

'I'm sorry about Mrs Turner,' she said slowly, honestly. 'But—oh, Laura, I can't help worrying. Not really for myself, but for my baby. We've been waiting so long, and hoping, and the other times, when we lost the babies, it was so awful. This time, everything seemed to be all right. I—I couldn't bear it if I lost my baby now!'

Laura took both Sally's hands in hers.

'You're not going to lose your baby, Sally,' she said firmly. 'You're fine, and the baby's fine, and even if it decided to be born now, it's big enough to do all right.'

Some of the shadows cleared from the other girl's eyes.

'And active enough,' she replied. 'I almost lost a cup of tea this morning when the baby kicked it!'

Then, with a determined effort, she smiled.

'Anyway, thanks to this situation, I can't do anything but rest, and that's good. Hey, you look as if you could do with some rest yourself, Laura.'

'I've just woken up,' Laura protested. 'I had quite a few hours sleep. I'm off tomorrow, though, and I plan on a good sleep, a good long walk, perhaps to see these Bushman paintings.'

Her grazed knee was almost better, a hot bath had taken most of the stiffness from it, and she felt that a good energetic walk up the steep mountain path would do her the world of good. Penny's condition remained stable, and Mrs Turner was no worse, so she felt that even if she couldn't put her patients right out of her mind, at least she could try, for a few hours, not to think about them.

The cave with the Bushman paintings was on the mountainside at the back of the Thornton House, and thus in the area they were free to go. Laura collected some fruit, and a bottle of orange juice, and a stout stick that Miss Durham offered her, and set off soon after ten. But the Matron was doubtful when she heard where Laura planned to go.

'I thought you were only going along the river,' she said. 'It's quite a long way to the cave, and there are clouds. The weather can change very quickly here in the Drakensberg, you know, my dear.'

There were clouds, but they were far over the pass.

'I'll be fine,' Laura said cheerfully. 'I walk a lot on Table Mountain, you know, and I'm a member of the Mountain Club.'

She set off down the path. Yes, there were some clouds. Perhaps she should put off this long walk, leave it for another time. It was never wise to ignore advice.

While she was considering this, she came to a clearing beside the river, and she was in it before the two people there saw her. They were sitting on a fallen log, talking, and as David looked down into Gwen Lund's vivid face, he was smiling. They were, Laura thought, strangely detached, very close together.

'Hello, Laura,' said David easily, rising to his feet unhurriedly. 'You look businesslike. I hope you're not going far, apparently the weather is going to change pretty quickly.'

Until that moment, Laura had almost decided to take Miss Durham's advice and change her mind about going to the Bushman cave. But her slow, rising anger and resentment at David Mackay made it impossible for her to do anything but reject his advice.

'I'm going to the Bushman cave,' she told him coolly. 'I'm not worried about the weather.'

'You could get pretty wet,' said Gwen Lund, and the amusement on her face made Laura even more determined.

'I won't melt,' she replied briefly, and, she knew, rather rudely.

Without saying goodbye, she walked on past them, and across the stepping-stones on the river. The path on the other side was steep, and she didn't look back at all, only pausing when she was round the corner and out of sight.

The path, although steep, was easy to follow, for every few yards there was a whitewashed stone. Laura climbed steadily, glad of the physical exertion, glad that she had to concentrate on where she was putting her feet, on conserving breath.

It was when she sat down and looked around that she realised, with dismay, that the few distant clouds now almost filled the sky. People did say the weather changed quickly in the Drakensberg, but—this quickly? Far down below, she could see Thornton House. Would it be wiser, she wondered, to turn now, and head down? But she was nearly at the cave, and she would have to admit to David Mackay, and to Gwen Lund, that she hadn't actually reached it.

No, darn it, she thought, I'm going on.

It was when she was between the overhanging rock and the cave, round the side of the mountain slope, that she felt the first drops of rain. Within minutes the heavens opened, and she was soaked. The path under her feet became instantly slippery and treacherous, and she had to grasp clumps of grass to keep herself from falling. But she could see the cave ahead of her, and as always with Bushman caves, it was well chosen for shelter, so she knew that the only thing she could do was to go on.

It wasn't a big cave, but once she was inside it she was sheltered from the rain and the wind, and the cold that had come with them. Not the first time I've been caught in the rain on a mountain walk, Laura told herself, and she searched in the small rucksack she had brought, for her extra jersey, a big loose one. It was dark in the cave, and she could barely see what she was doing, but it seemed to make sense to strip off her soaking shirt and jersey, and even her bra, before she pulled on the other jersey, which was damp, but more comfortable than the other clothes, which had been completely soaked. As well as she could, she rubbed her hair and dried her face, before going cautiously towards the mouth of the cave and looking out.

The rain was a solid sheet of water now, and the path she had come up looked like a stream itself. She wished, for the first time, that her anger at David Mackay—and at the girl with him—hadn't made her behave in a way that she had to admit had been foolish. Now she would have to wait here until the rain stopped, and the path became a possibility again. At the very least, she thought, she'd probably catch cold, and that would teach her a lesson.

She retreated a little and sat down on the floor of the cave to eat an apple. It would probably be a long wait, and she was cold and wet and uncomfortable, but she'd just have to put up with that.

In the cave, it was too dark for her to see her watch, so she had no idea how long she had been there before she saw the flash of lightning, outlined against the mouth of the cave, and then, only a second later, there was a roll of thunder. Very close—almost overhead, she realised, and she clasped her hands together to steady them. All her life she had been afraid of thunder and lightning. But there had always, before, been a safe place to go, someone to talk to, to help her to conquer her fears.

Now she was alone on a mountainside, in a dark and gloomy cave, and all around her the thunder rolled, and the lightning flashed, and unreasoning terror filled her whole body. She began to cry, unable to stop herself.

In the ominous silence between two crashes of thunder, she heard something else, and there, at the mouth of the cave, was a figure.

She screamed.

'Laura!'

There was a flash of lightning, and she saw that it was David Mackay. And then a dreadful crash of thunder, right overhead.

She screamed again, and beyond thought, ran into the arms of the man she was so sure she hated. Even in her terror she could feel his surprise as she hurtled herself against him, and then his arms closed around her.

'It's all right, Laura, it's all right.'

Beyond these words, she heard nothing of what he was saying, she knew only that she wasn't alone, that his voice was comforting and his arms were reassuring. Outside, the storm still raged, but here in the shelter of the cave it was dry and safe.

Slowly she regained control of herself.

'I'm sorry,' she managed to say at last, unevenly. 'I've always hated storms, and this is such a terrible one.' For the first time, the reason for his presence came home to her, and she turned to him in the darkness. 'Did you come after me?' she asked him.

She felt him nod.

'I could see the storm up here, and I knew it was going to be a bad one,' he said. 'Laura, you really are a very foolish girl, to be disregarding advice. I believe Miss Durham told you you'd be better not to go to the cave.' His arm was still round her shoulders, and when there was another crash of thunder, she moved closer to him, with no thought, only instinct. 'And even I could see it wasn't a good idea, the way the clouds were building up. Are you always so stubborn?'

How could she tell him that she had made a foolish, childish decision, because she had been angry at seeing him with Gwen Lund? No, that wasn't it, she thought, dismissing the thought, I just—didn't like everyone telling me.

'I didn't realise it was going to change so quickly,' she explained, not too steadily. 'I'm sorry you had to come.'

'So am I,' he replied. 'There's plenty more for you and me to be doing, rather than sitting in a cave, and both of us cold and wet. I didn't expect such irresponsible behaviour from you, Laura.'

It had been irresponsible, there was no getting round that. And he was right, here they were both stuck in this cave, when they might be needed down at the little hospital in the hills.

'I really am sorry,' she said, her voice low. 'I should have had more sense. I should—'

And then, as she was speaking, there was a jagged flash of lightning across the mouth of the cave, and a booming crash of thunder at the same moment. Unable to stop herself, Laura turned to the arms of the man beside her.

This time he said nothing. But his arms closed around her and held her tightly, once again comforting her. He had taken his wet anorak off, and his thick jersey was warm and reasonably dry, and slowly, surely, her terror subsided. His arms were still around her, and now, in the darkness, his lips found hers.

This time there was immediate urgency and demand in his kiss, and this time, with no thought, no warning, she was responding to him with every fibre of her being, unable to stop herself, wanting nothing in the world but this man's arms around her, his lips on hers.

CHAPTER NINE

AFTERWARDS, each time Laura remembered that kiss in the darkness of the mountain cave, shame filled her, for it was David who drew back first, David whose lips left hers, when she would have clung to him.

'I'm giving you fair warning,' he said unsteadily, 'that pretty soon I'm going to forget any good intentions I ever had, and—'

He was still very close to her, and she could hear, now, from his voice, that he was smiling.

'You're quite a lass, Laura,' he said softly. 'I don't think I'll ever understand you in a hundred years, but I will surely enjoy trying to.'

Slowly, sanity was returning. She drew back from him, and took a deep, ragged breath.

'I don't know what to say,' she began, with difficulty. 'But I think we should go just as soon as we can. The storm seems to be easing off a bit, and we're wet already, so it doesn't matter if it's still raining.'

In the darkness his hand found hers and closed on it, but Laura, as if she had been burned, pulled her hand back.

'No—leave me alone!'

There was silence—a long silence.

'I've heard of girls like you,' David said at last, evenly. 'But I've been lucky enough not to meet one until now.' And then the cool remoteness was gone from his voice. 'Laura, lass, what is it? Each time I think I'm getting close to you, you put up this damned barrier, this wall.'

She could feel his breath warm on her cheek, and she turned away.

'Let's just forget it,' she said quickly, lightly. 'Look, I was frightened—I hate storms. I—didn't know what I was doing, I was so glad to see someone—anyone.'

There was another silence.

'So anyone would have got that reception, I take it?' he asked. 'I just happened to be the lucky guy.'

In the darkness, she felt warm colour flood her cheeks, and she was glad he couldn't see her. She said nothing.

And then, disconcertingly, his voice was warm.

'Why won't you give us a chance, Laura?' he asked her. 'I'm sticking my neck out, but why won't you admit there's something between us? Or there could be, if you would only give it a chance.'

Never in all her life had Laura felt the way she had in this man's arms. But how could she have responded so eagerly to a man she didn't even like? How could her body have behaved so treacherously?

And once again shame brought a flood of colour to her cheeks, when she remembered that it had been David who had drawn back, when she would have clung to him, when she would have been unable to do anything but go along with the tide of passion engulfing her.

Ashamed, and panic-stricken at the violence and the depth of her reaction to David's kiss, Laura wanted nothing now but to get out of here, away from him.

'I'd rather not discuss this any more,' she said clearly. 'I don't know about you, but I'm going down before it gets any worse.' And she stood up.

David followed her to the mouth of the cave.

'As you wish,' he agreed, his voice expressionless. 'Personally, I feel that if we give it half an hour the rain will have stopped, but I can see you find my company in a place like this unacceptable. Here, you'd better have my anorak, I don't think you have much on under that jersey, and it's pretty cold.'

Laura was glad to turn away and pick up the soaking shirt and bra she had taken off when she first reached the cave. She stuffed them into her rucksack, and when the big doctor held out his anorak to her, she accepted it without a word.

The path was muddy and treacherous, and Laura, walking down behind David, slipped more than once. But he didn't look round at all, until they reached the first river crossing. To her dismay, the stepping-stones she had so easily come across had almost disappeared.

'I'll give you a hand,' said David brusquely. 'Remember, the stones will be very slippery now, so take care. I'll go ahead and test them.'

When he had reached the second stone, he turned back and held out his hand to her. Laura had no choice but to put her hand in his and let him steady her until she was on the first stone. He moved on then, and helped her to the next stone. When they reached the other side he let go of her hand and walked on again, without looking back. It was still raining heavily, and there was an occasional flash of lightning and a distant peal of thunder, but the storm had moved further away now. It was only when they reached the garden at Thornton House that David stopped, and looked down at her.

'I would suggest that you have a hot bath, and something hot to drink,' he said remotely. 'I plan on doing the same. Neither of us can afford to catch a chill, we're both needed.'

Laura's throat felt very tight.

'I'm very sorry,' she said, her voice low. 'It was foolish of me to go up there, and have you coming up to rescue me. Thank you for doing that.'

His eyes were very dark.

'The foolishness I can forgive,' he said, unsmiling. 'The rest—I would be finding it harder. Take that bath, please.'

He left her then, without another word, his tall figure striding round the side of the big house. Laura went in the back door, so that she could leave some of her wet clothes in the porch, then hurried to her room, glad to reach there without meeting anyone. Particularly, she had to admit, the dark-haired Gwen Lund, who had been with David when she set off in the morning. She ran a hot bath, and as she lay in it, she thought that the morning seemed very far away.

She dressed in her uniform right away, for it was almost time for the daily staff conference. When she went in, David nodded to her briefly, and then, having checked that everyone was there, he began his report.

'We have another patient,' he said abruptly. 'Mr Wood's blood test shows that he has contracted the virus too. His symptoms are slight at the moment, but there's no doubt that the test is positive, and once again we're hitting it with everything. He is now, of course, in the isolation unit. The news from Cape Town is not too good—another two suspected cases, and a deterioration in the condition of some of the confirmed cases.'

Even one extra patient increased the work load, but Laura's main concern, over the next hours, was an undoubted deterioration in Penny's condition.

David, studying Penny's chart, met her eyes for a moment, then beckoned her out of the room.

'I don't like the clinical picture,' he told her. 'There are signs of kidney problems now. Let me know if anything worries you about any of them.'

There was no need for her to send for him, for the condition of the three patients remained stable, but when Laura went off duty there was a message from him, asking her to go to his office.

She went with some trepidation, but David was completely and entirely professional. As, of course, she would have expected him to be, she reminded herself hastily.

'Ah, Sister Kent,' he said, looking up from his desk. 'I won't be a moment.'

He finished what he was writing and put it aside. Then he looked up at her pleasantly, impersonally.

'I'm going to be away from here for about three days,' he told her. 'I'm going to New York to see Ted Newton, and I'm going to do everything in my power to persuade him to let us have the antidote he's working on. I've been in research myself, and I know his problems, I know what he'll say. But we're getting nowhere with Dr Marsh speaking to him on the telephone, so this is worth trying.' His dark eyes were bleak all at once. 'If he does agree, I just hope we're in time. Oh—one other thing. Your friend Dr Sheldon is coming here while I'm away.' He looked at his watch. 'In fact, he should be here in an hour, and I'll have to be ready to leave on the helicopter that brings him.'

He stood up.

'I'm sure I can rely on all the team here working well with Dr Sheldon in my absence,' he said pleasantly.

Laura couldn't help looking at him with suspicion, but his eyes met hers coolly, levelly. Somewhat at a loss, and annoyed with herself for feeling like that, she murmured something, and went out of the room.

In an hour, the helicopter would be here, he had said. For some reason that she didn't want to go into too deeply, Laura was reluctant to be around when Jeff arrived, to be greeted by him while David watched. Knowing Jeff, he was quite likely to ignore any professional etiquette and lift her off her feet in a hug, or give her an exuberant kiss. But perhaps it would look even more strange, she thought, if she stayed away.

She went to her room, changed into jeans and a sweater, and was just going along the corridor when she heard the sound of the helicopter. The lawn of Thornton House was big enough for it to land on, since this was only a three-seater, and there was a small group of people already waiting. David was there, casually dressed in jeans and a suede jacket, with a small suitcase at his feet. Gwen Lund was beside him talking to him animatedly. For a moment, Laura wished she could turn and go back inside, but it was too late. And Gwen Lund's eyes were on her, amused, interested. And—challenging, in some way, Laura thought, disturbed.

With relief, she saw Irene, and went to join her.

'Hi, stranger—seems ages since I've seen you,' she said, and she was smiling, but Laura could see the strain and the shadows in her eyes.

'I know,' she agreed. 'Our off duty times just haven't connected.'

'Time for a coffee after this lot is clear?' asked Irene, and Laura nodded her agreement.

The helicopter had landed, and Jeff Sheldon swung himself down. David Mackay stepped forward, and the two doctors shook hands. Then David drew Jeff back towards the house, and away from the sound of the helicopter. Laura, relieved, was about to turn and go off with Irene when she saw Jeff put a hand on the other man's arm, then turn and come towards her. So he had seen her, in that moment before David greeted him. She hadn't been sure.

There was nothing she could do but wait, and wonder what Jeff would do.

But Jeff didn't do any of the things she had half expected he would. He came right up to her, took both her hands in his for a moment, and looked down at her.

'I'll see you later, Laura,' he told her. 'I've got to talk to the big boss now. Hello, Irene, nice to see you again.'

He turned and walked back to where David was standing still, waiting. And watching, Laura thought. Strange for Jeff to be quiet, restrained, like that. She was relieved, but at the same time it bothered her, for there had been something very—intense, intimate, almost, in what he had done. And David must have seen.

Not that it mattered to her what David Mackay saw or thought, she reminded herself quickly.

'Time for that coffee now?' asked Irene. 'Or do you want to wait and see Jeff?'

Laura shook her head.

She and Irene were in Irene's room, waiting for the kettle to boil, when they heard the helicopter take off.

'I hope he comes back with the antidote,' murmured Laura. She and Irene looked at each other, and there was no need for either of them to speak about Penny, lying silent and still in the isolation room.

'Nothing else seems to help,' Irene said after a while, handing Laura a mug of coffee.

'No one knows enough about this virus,' Laura reminded her. 'Dr Mackay has been hitting it with everything there is, but any mutation has problems. All we can say is that in the patients who are still alive, we're holding it at bay, but no more. That's why Dr Mackay has to get this antidote. We need to be able to do more than just hold it at bay.' She stirred her coffee, and turned to her friend. 'How are things with you and Pieter?' she asked.

Irene shrugged.

'Much the same. Thanks for looking in on him, it must be pretty boring having to stay in your room when you feel well enough to go out.' And then the forced lightness of her voice was gone. 'I daren't let myself think of him getting this virus, after the treatment he's had, and the low resistance because of his illness.' For a moment her hand touched Laura's. 'Thanks, anyway, Laura.'

'I've done very little,' shrugged Laura. 'Just popped in when I could.' She hesitated. 'Irene, I haven't felt, yet, that I could talk to him about the two of you. We're still getting to know each other.'

Irene smiled, but it was a smile that didn't reach her eyes.

'I can understand that, Laura,' she replied. 'It's not very realistic of me to have asked you, but I thought he might listen to you, where he won't listen to me.' She set her cup down. 'It's funny, he's very practical and realistic about his illness, he's asked for the truth all along, and he knows how things are. He'll go along with anything the doctors think might help, but he isn't looking for miracles. He's very clear-sighted about all this, and yet he won't accept that we should get married now, and make the most of whatever time is left. He keeps saying it isn't fair to me.'

She brushed the back of her hand across her eyes, and Laura's heart ached for her.

'I'll try to talk to him, Irene,' she promised. 'Perhaps you're right, and talking to someone else could help.'

Irene stood up.

'I'm on duty, have to rush,' she said, and dried one stray tear that had rolled down her cheek. 'Thanks, Laura, I needed company. And sympathy.'

Jeff was obviously busy at the isolation ward, and Laura didn't see him until later that evening. She had just finished having dinner before going on duty when she saw him come into the small dining-room and stride across to her.

'I'm just off and you're just on,' he said ruefully. 'What a life!' He slid into the seat beside her and looked at her, and once again there was that intensity in his eyes that had already disturbed her.

'I can't talk to you here, Laura,' he said, his voice low. 'Let's get out of here, if you've finished.'

'I'm just going on duty, I haven't much time,' Laura reminded him.

'I know that,' he replied. 'Just five minutes on our own.'

She gave in then and went with him along the corridor to the small sitting-room, deserted now. As it had been that night she had come in and found David Mackay here, she thought, and wished she hadn't remembered that night.

She sat down on the couch, and Jeff sat beside her.

'Laura, before you left, I tried to pin you down,' he began, with a seriousness that she had never seen in him before. 'We've known each other a long time, and I guess we've kind of drifted on. Well, I was beginning to realise that wasn't what I wanted, and this has really brought it home to me.' Again, as he had done that morning, he took both her hands in his. 'Laura, love,

I've missed you so much. I don't know why it's taken me so long to get there, but—I love you, Laura. I want us to be married.'

Laura tried to free her hands, but he wouldn't release her. He was looking at her, waiting for her to say something.

'Oh, Jeff,' she said, a little shakily, unable to hide her dismay, 'Jeff, not here, not now. I—I can't think about anything like that just now.'

His blue eyes were steady, and there was a new determination in his face.

'I realise that, Laura,' he replied. 'Maybe I shouldn't have said anything, but I had to let you know how I feel. I do accept that this isn't the right time or place, but I'll wait.'

'No, Jeff, don't say that,' she protested, distressed, almost overcome by a sensation of being trapped, slowly and steadily. 'I don't think—'

He released her hands, and put a finger over her lips.

'Don't say it,' he told her. 'Don't say no, because I won't accept that.'

He stood up.

'All right, I'm not going to say any more now, I know it's time you were going on duty.' He looked down at her. 'There's only one more thing, Laura.'

He kissed her then, his lips warm on hers. But she knew that he sensed her lack of response, because after a moment he drew back. His eyes searched her face, questioning, then he told her that he could understand that all her thoughts were on Penny, and the other patients.

'Like I said, I can wait,' he finished.

Laura went along the corridor to start work, troubled, but not knowing what to do about Jeff. And unable to stop herself wondering whether it really was only because this was the wrong time, the wrong place, that she had so many doubts.

In some ways, she was glad to be very busy, glad to have no time to think of anything but her work and her patients. She had to keep a constant check on Penny, to watch for any breathing problems, and now, as well, for any possibility of kidney failure. Most of the time Penny was unconscious, and even when she stirred and moved, restlessly, she didn't recognise anyone. There was little Laura could do other than try to keep her comfortable, and do the tests David needed done.

Mrs Turner, too, had to be watched, as there was a real danger of her heart being strained. She was good and uncomplaining, although the bad headaches that all the patients had bothered her considerably.

'I'm sorry to keep complaining, Sister,' she said apologetically, 'but I can't seem to get rid of this headache, no matter how many pills and injections you give me. Maybe this new thing the doctor has gone for will help.'

'And how do you know about that, Mrs Turner?' Laura asked, and the old woman coloured.

'Well, I did just hear him talking to the other Sister,' she answered defensively.

Harry Wood was asleep, and Laura was grateful for that. She hadn't liked the man from the start, and what she had seen of him when he tried to get away had only confirmed that. But he was a patient, and she was a nurse, and likes and dislikes didn't count.

It was strange, working with Jeff instead of with David Mackay. Jeff was a good doctor, she had always known that, but there was no doubt that David was something special. As a doctor, she reminded herself quickly. The patients felt it too. Even in this short time they had become dependent on him.

'It's not the same without Dr Mackay,' Mrs Turner whispered to Laura the following day, when Jeff had just gone out. 'Don't you think so, Sister?'

Laura busied herself writing on Mrs Turner's chart.

'Dr Sheldon is very good, Mrs Turner,' she answered. 'And he's been working at St Luke's since this whole thing started, so he does know what he's doing.'

'Oh, I'm sure he does, dear,' the old woman agreed. 'But he just isn't the same. I do like my Scottish doctor!'

Because they were so busy, Laura had no chance to go and see Pieter van Heerden, as she had promised Irene she would. She was sorry about that, but she was glad there was no time for her to see Jeff. He was busy and she was busy, and that was fine. She knew that they would have to talk before long, but she needed time to think, time to work out just what she did feel about Jeff.

Before the three days were up, David was back. There was a message from Durban to say he was on the way, and soon the hum of the small army helicopter was heard coming down the valley towards Thornton House.

Everyone who could be there, it seemed, was outside waiting as the helicopter landed. Laura and Jill Derry, the other Sister, stood with Jeff Sheldon, and watched as the door opened and David swung himself down, looked around swiftly, and came towards them.

He looks so tired, Laura thought immediately. Tired, and—

But there was no need to wonder, for as he reached them, he smiled.

'I've got it,' he told them. 'Ted Newton needed a fair bit of persuading, because he feels there's a lot more testing to be done, but I've gone over his tests, and I'm satisfied we can go ahead and try it. Dr Marsh is putting his patients at St Luke's on to it immediately, and we're going to do the same.'

For a moment, it seemed to Laura, his eyes held hers.

'But we mustn't forget that it's risky, using a new drug,' he said soberly. 'Very risky.'

CHAPTER TEN

THE whole medical team knew there would be no immediate reaction to the new drug, the antidote David Mackay had flown to America to get. And yet Laura found herself, half an hour after the doctor had given all three patients an injection, checking and re-checking, hoping, although she knew it was too early, for some change in the clinical picture.

'There's nothing we can do now but wait, Sister Kent,' David Mackay said from behind her, as she took Penny's temperature. 'And don't be thinking this is a miracle drug Newton has developed. He won't make any claims for it, certainly not at this stage.'

She followed him out of the room, and they both took off their masks.

'He's had positive results in the lab,' the doctor said, almost to himself. 'But we're now part of his testing system, because our patients here, and the patients at St Luke's, are the first human patients to be given the antidote. We have to remember, too, that each mutation of Congo or Lassa or Marburg, is different from the others.' He smiled, then, and the lines of weariness were gone. 'But having said all that, we'll all be hoping and praying.'

His eyes met hers.

'You're surprised that I say praying?' he asked her, and she coloured, uncomfortable that he had so quickly known what she was thinking. 'You know, Sister Kent, you and I, and all the other folks with all their medical training, can do a great deal. But not everything. We can't be relying entirely on ourselves. We need all the help we can get, and I know of no other way to get it.'

When he had gone, Laura went slowly back into the intensive care room. Something else, she thought, to surprise her, to bring her up short, about this man. And suddenly, with a forlorn emptiness that shook her, she found herself thinking that so long ago, it seemed, she had thought she knew this man. Now she just kept on finding that in fact she didn't know him at all.

Jeff Sheldon had stayed on for one more day, to hand over to David, and he had said he would like to stay longer, until there was some positive reaction to the new drug. But there was a message from Dr Marsh in Cape Town, saying they needed him there, and an hour later the Army helicopter would take him to Durban, so that he could connect with a Cape Town flight.

Laura had just come off duty when Jeff came looking for her, to tell her this.

'Nice to know I'm needed,' he said lightly, but she could see that he was disappointed to be going now. Partly because he wanted to see the effects of the drugs on the patients here, of course, but partly, she knew, because of her. And because she knew that, she hoped she had been able to hide the relief she felt.

'I'll come out and wait with you,' she told him. 'When is the helicopter due to arrive?'

'Any time now,' he said. 'I'm packed and ready, so I came to see you.'

They had reached the door and Laura went out, unwilling to be alone with Jeff if she could help it, and hoping there would be other people there waiting for the helicopter, and the supplies and the mail it would bring at the same time.

But the only person outside was Gwen Lund, and Laura's feelings were mixed as the girl came towards them.

'So they're sending you back so soon, Jeff,' she said, barely glancing at Laura. 'You've hardly been here any time at all.'

Long enough, Laura thought, with a dislike that surprised her, for you to get on to first-name terms. But I shouldn't think that would take you too long.

'Yes, I hoped I'd have a little longer,' Jeff replied. He smiled, pleasantly. 'Look, Gwen, I don't want to be rude, but Laura and I have a couple of things to talk about. Do you mind?'

'Not at all,' the girl said, very sweetly. 'I'm sure Laura would do the same for me, wouldn't you, Laura?'

And she walked across the lawn to sit on a garden seat under the big oak tree.

'Laura,' said Jeff, looking down at her, 'I know you're going to say you can't give me an answer yet, but surely this will all be over soon, and you'll be back in Cape Town. I just want you to think about it. We've always had fun together, and we've always got on well, and—you know now how I feel about you.'

Laura turned away, disturbed by this new intensity in his eyes. Theirs had always been a light, fairly casual relationship. Somehow she had never thought of it changing, never thought of Jeff looking at her like this.

'Jeff,' she said slowly, troubled, 'I know all that, but I don't think I'm ready to think about marriage. Couldn't we just let things go on as they are for a bit?'

It was a moment or two before he replied.

'I don't think so, Laura,' he said at last. 'Please think about what I've said, and I'll be waiting for you to come back to Cape Town.'

Above them the helicopter was circling, making ready to land. Jeff tried to say something else, but she had to shake her head, because she couldn't hear him. By the time the landing was done, and the volume of sound lowered, David was with them, holding out his hand to Jeff.

'Thanks for all you've done, Jeff,' he said. 'I'm sorry you'll miss out on seeing the progress here, but you'll be in on it at the other end. I think perhaps we should—'

He stopped, for Gwen Lund had joined them, and her hand was on his arm, lightly, but possessively, Laura couldn't help thinking.

'David,' she said reproachfully, 'I'm sure you interrupted Jeff saying goodbye to Laura. That wasn't very tactful of you, now was it?'

David looked at Laura for a moment, and then at Jeff.

'No, I don't suppose it was,' he agreed, and his voice was low. 'Thanks anyway, Jeff. And—sorry.'

He turned away, then, and walked back to the house, with Gwen beside him. Jeff put his arms around Laura and held her close for a moment, before his lips touched hers briefly, warmly.

'Remember,' he murmured, 'I'm waiting for that answer, and it has to be the right answer.'

When he had left her, and walked across to the helicopter, Laura wanted to go inside right away, to busy herself with something—anything—so that she could put Jeff out of her mind. But she knew he would be watching, and she made herself stand there on the lawn as the helicopter rose, and wave as it made a wide turn

turn to head away from the mountains and the pass.

Only then did she turn and walk towards the door of Thornton House.

David was there waiting for her.

'I have a request from Sally Benson,' he told her. 'She says if you have time, please look in and see her. I think she's feeling a bit low.' He looked at his watch. 'Maybe when you come on duty again, we'll be seeing something happening.'

There was kindness and concern in his eyes, even after what had happened between them on the mountain—and that disturbed her even more than the way Jeff had looked at her.

'I'll go and see Sally,' she said, more abruptly than she had meant to, and she turned and went towards the other wing of the house, where the only patients left now were Sally, and Pieter van Heerden.

When she knocked on the door and went in, Sally's face lit up, but not before Laura had seen the shadows under her eyes, the slightly drawn look of her face.

She told Sally about Jeff going back to Cape Town, and she told her that yes, they were waiting to see if the American drug was going to be successful, and they should know fairly soon. And as they talked, and she answered Sally's questions, she was looking at the girl unobtrusively, professionally.

'How are you feeling, Sally?' she asked at last, lightly.

The blue eyes clouded.

'A little peculiar,' Sally said carefully. 'I think it's just discomfort—indigestion, probably, but do you think Dr Mackay could check things, and make sure everything is all right?' She smiled, but the smile didn't quite reach her eyes. 'No hurry, just when he can.'

Laura stood up.

'I'll pop along and ask him now,' she replied, her voice as casual as Sally's own.

But David wasn't in his office. Laura left a note for him, asking him if he would mind having a look at Sally as soon as he could, and then she went back to sit with Sally.

'I'll sit with you for a bit longer,' she offered, although she had planned on going in to see Pieter van Heerden.

But Sally shook her head.

'I must finish this letter to Neil—it's tough for him, me being stuck here, and he doesn't really know what's going on. And we're only allowed such short phone calls, in case the line is needed. No, you go and see Irene's young man, he probably needs cheering up much more than I do.'

Pieter van Heerden was sitting at the window, and he turned when she went in.

'Here are some more magazines,' said Laura. 'And I think some new books came in with the supplies, so I'll see what I can find, and Irene can bring them to you.'

'Thanks,' the young man said. 'I could use something more to read.' He looked at her, steadily, then taking her by surprise, he said, 'I suppose Irene asked you to talk to me, to try to persuade me to see things her way.'

Laura sat down on the other chair. There was, she thought, no point in denying that. There was something very clear-sighted about Pieter, something that made pretence of any kind unnecessary.

'Yes, she did,' she replied quietly.

'You're wasting your time,' he told her firmly. 'Can you think of anything more foolish for a girl like Irene than to marry a man who might be dead in a few months?'

Laura took a deep breath.

'Yes, I can,' she said clearly. 'And that's for a girl like Irene to spend the rest of her life wishing she'd had these months, or years, or whatever, with the man she loved.'

She could see that Pieter was taken aback by this, and she leaned forward. If he's going to be hard-hitting, I'll be too, she decided.

'Do you think that just because you're not married, these next months are going to be any easier for Irene?' she asked him. 'And do you think that the lack of a wedding ring will make her grieving less hard, afterwards?'

He turned away.

'It seems such a useless thing to do,' he said, his voice low. 'Marriage means a future, and I have no future.'

Laura hesitated, but only for a moment.

'I'm sure you know the prognosis as well as I do,' she said. 'But you must know too that this period of remission could go on longer than you or the doctors think. Wouldn't it be worthwhile being together, for whatever time you do have?'

'I don't want Irene's pity,' Pieter told her tightly.

Laura lost patience.

'For heaven's sake, Pieter, you don't have Irene's pity, you have her love!' she snapped, more sharply than she had meant to.

For a moment their eyes locked. She thought he was going to turn away, his face closed, his mind and his heart closed, but then, with difficulty, he smiled.

'You pack quite a punch, Laura,' he said, surprisingly. 'Now go and leave me in peace—I have some thinking to do.'

Outside his door, Laura paused. She didn't want to be too hopeful, but maybe, just maybe, she had given him something to think about.

She was on the point of going back to the other wing when she saw David striding along towards her, his white coat flying.

'I got your note,' he said. 'Has she started?'

Laura shook her head.

'No, no contractions, but I'm not entirely happy about her.' She hesitated and then said, apologetically, 'It's really just a feeling.'

She thought, for a moment, that he was going to show annoyance at her asking him to come because of a feeling, but he smiled and said he sometimes had feelings about patients too, and it was wiser not to ignore them.

'Come in with me,' he asked her, and they went in together, Laura standing by while the doctor examined Sally, and checked the foetal heart.

'You're fine, and so is the baby,' he told her at last. 'He's active, and he's in the right position, but at this moment he's not showing any signs of putting in an appearance soon. So relax, walk around your room, sit at the open window and get some fresh air, and try not to worry.'

As they walked along the corridor together, he turned to Laura.

'I have that feeling too,' he said abruptly. 'Have you done midwifery, Laura? And has Jill Derry?'

'I have,' Laura told him. 'Jill hasn't, she's planning to do it next year.'

David nodded.

'I may have to ask you to help me, if she does go into labour,' he said.

Just then his bleeper sounded, and he had to take a phone call from Cape Town.

'Wait—it might be good news,' he said to Laura, before hurrying ahead of her into his office. Laura, a little hesitantly, did wait outside, and a few moments later he came out.

'There's a definite improvement in almost all the patients in St Luke's,' he told her. 'Nothing dramatic, and it looks as if it will be slow, but something is happening.' He looked at his watch. 'Let's see, the people in St Luke's had their first injection at least six hours before our peopl   here, so it will still be some time. But it's something, isn't it?'

'It certainly is,' Laura agreed soberly.

In spite of the timing he had worked out she couldn't help, when she went on duty later, looking hopefully at all three patients. But there was no change in any of them, although now, with this news, David had asked for hourly temperatures to be taken. Penny's tracheotomy tube had to be adjusted, and old Mrs Turner was nauseous, and Harry Wood, undoubtedly ill now, had to be convinced that there was no need for Dr Mackay to be sent for immediately.

All in all, Laura's time on duty flew past, and when she was going off, she had time for only a last quick glance at Penny's face, still and white, as she wondered if she would see a change when she came on duty next.

With all these things happening, she had forgotten about the possibility of Sally Benson going into labour, so she was completely bewildered to be wakened, just after midnight, by David shaking her shoulder.

'Laura, wake up—Sally's in labour, and I need your help,' he said. 'I knocked, but you didn't hear, so I came in. Are you awake now?'

Laura was thoroughly awake.

'Yes—I'll be with you in five minutes,' she told him.

'Good girl,' he said, and the approval in his eyes when she actually shortened that to four minutes pleased her, although she preferred not to dwell on that reaction.

'We'll have to use her own room for the delivery,' he said briskly. 'I've already got the incubator here, because I think Sally's going to have this baby in one big hurry!'

Laura, following him into the room and seeing Sally doing her breathing through a contraction, had to agree. It was uncommon with a first baby, but it could happen, and it had, that in the time since David had examined Sally before, she was now fully dilated.

'Easy, Sally, that's the way, hold back until we tell you,' said the doctor. 'Remember, when you push, don't push in your throat, that doesn't do anything. This little fellow is in such a hurry that a couple of pushes should do it.' His voice changed. 'Right, Sally, push!'

With the first push, the head crowned, and there was only a moment of respite for the girl on the bed, and then she bore down again. Gently, David and Laura eased the tiny shoulders, and then, with a swift and slippery movement, the baby was born.

'Clamp, Sister,' ordered David. 'Give it to me, and you take the baby. Hey, Sally, I was right—it's a boy!'

'Is he all right?' asked the young mother, and Laura, with the baby wrapped in a blanket, showed him to her.

'He's fine,' she said. 'He isn't even so small, for being born two or three weeks early, but we'll put him in the incubator, just as a precaution.'

David, having clamped the cord, examined the baby thoroughly now, smiling at the force of the crying from the tiny red-faced scrap.

'Hey, you're a smart little boy, coming along so quickly,' he said, 'and not even one stitch for your mummy! I bet your daddy will be thrilled with you. Incubator ready, Laura—Sister Kent?'

When the baby was in the incubator, he turned to her.

'I'm very glad you suggested we get this,' he told her, quietly. 'I think in a couple of days he'll do very nicely out of it, but that was good thinking.'

He moved over to the bed.

'Sister Kent will freshen you up, Sally, and then you'd probably like to get on to the phone to your husband, tell him he's got a son, and everything is fine.'

By the time the phone call was made, Miss Durham appeared, with a pot of tea.

'It's like a party,' said Sally, as they all sat drinking tea. 'In the middle of the night, too.'

'It is a party,' Laura pointed out. 'A birthday party! And now you can have a good long sleep, since Miss Durham is going to look after your baby.'

She and David walked along the corridor together, neither of them saying anything. Laura thought he was probably tired too, but somehow the silence between them was friendly, unstrained. She had found it absurdly touching, that he should speak to the baby as he had, and she found she couldn't stop thinking about it.

'Should we go and tell Sister Derry about the baby?' he asked, as they reached their own wing. 'And perhaps there might be some news from her, too.'

He had left instructions, he told her, that he wanted to be called if there was any change in any of the three patients, but he didn't expect anything for an hour or two yet.

'But since we're here, let's check,' he said.

Jill Derry was sitting at the small desk, writing, with the table lamp a small pool of light around her, and the rest of the room dim. She looked up, surprised, when David knocked on the window beside her.

'Dr Mackay—Laura!' she exclaimed.

'We've just had a baby,' David told her. 'Sally Benson has had a wee boy.'

Jill looked at Laura and smiled.

'Well, now I do believe you're given some sixth sense with that midwifery training,' she said. 'From what you told me earlier, there didn't seem to be any real reason for thinking she might deliver this soon. How is she? And the baby?'

Laura told her about the easy delivery, and the good condition of both mother and baby, and it was only when she had finished that she saw the suppressed excitement on the other girl's face.

'I was just going to bleep you, Dr Mackay,' said Jill.

'Penny?' Laura asked, not quite steadily.

Jill's grey eyes were compassionate.

'No, not Penny. At least, not yet.' She turned to the doctor. 'Mr Wood's temperature has dropped. Only a degree, but it does mean something, surely.'

David Mackay studied the chart she held out to him.

'I think it does,' he said quietly. 'We've been trying to get that temperature down for days, and nothing has moved it. And it makes sense, that he's the first one to show improvement, since he's the least ill. They have all had their second shot, now, surely in a few hours we'll see a change with the others too.' He smiled down at Laura. 'Time you were back in bed, Sister Kent— once your patients start recovering, you could have an even busier time!'

At the end of the corridor leading to the isolation unit, they both stopped, as Laura's room was in one direction, and his in the other. All around them everything was still, and hushed, and Laura couldn't help feeling that in spite of everything, the birth they had just shared in was somehow a bond between them.

'Goodnight, Laura,' said David softly.

Laura. This wasn't the first time, tonight, he had said that. But until now it had been Sister Kent, correct and professional, because of what had happened between them in the cave. Because of what she had said.

She hesitated, but only for a moment.

'Goodnight, David,' she replied.

She thought for a moment that he was about to say something else, but he only looked down at her for a long time, so long that she felt uncomfortable under the steady directness of his dark eyes. And then, very softly, he said goodnight again, and left her.

CHAPTER ELEVEN

THE following morning there was no doubt that the American antidote was having an effect on their patients.

Harry Wood's temperature was almost normal, although he still had the aching limbs and the headache that had been the early symptoms. Mrs Turner, too was responding, although more slowly, and they would, David said soberly, have to watch all the time for any signs that her heart was affected, either by the strain of the illness, or by the antidote itself.

Penny hadn't yet regained consciousness, but they had been able to remove the tracheotomy tube, and she was breathing normally. Laura, who had always before been able to assess a patient's condition with professional distance, found that with Penny she was unable to do this. She thought her friend's colour was slightly better, and that there was a less unhealthy feel to her skin, but she could not rely on her own judgement, and apart from a minimal drop in temperature, there was yet no clinical change, other than with her breathing.

David, examining Penny carefully, methodically, looked up at last.

'I think she's stabilised,' he said. 'The improvement has begun, and I think it's going to continue.'

He stood up and stretched, and when he went out of the room he beckoned Laura to follow him.

'I thought we were going to lose her,' he said, almost to himself. 'And I think we would have, if it hadn't been

for that antidote, if we hadn't been able to overcome
Dr Newton's scruples. Which reminds me—I have a
couple of hours of work ahead of me, writing up our
findings here, so they can be used in America to help
the research folk. We owe them that, don't we?'

'We certainly do,' Laura agreed.

She looked at him and saw that he was very tired.
And because of the closeness there had been between
them last night, when they delivered Sally Benson's
baby, she was able to say to him that perhaps he should
leave the writing-up for the moment, and go to bed
instead.

'I'm fine,' he told her, dismissing this. 'Just jet-lag,
I think. I'm going to check on Sally and the baby now,
though, before I get into this. Are you off now?'

Laura looked at her watch.

'Yes, Jill should be here any minute, then I'm off.'

David smiled, the slow, warm smile she felt, somehow, she had always known.

'Then I'll wait, and we can go along together.'

Ten minutes later, with Jill Derry in charge of the
patients, Laura joined him, and they walked along
towards the other wing.

'Jill thinks Penny looks better too,' she told him.

He glanced down at her.

'Glad to have my judgement confirmed,' he said
lightly.

Laura coloured.

'I didn't mean that,' she told him. 'It's just—I'm glad
of anyone saying that, bolstering up my lack of confidence in my own feelings.'

Outside Sally's door, he stopped.

'I can understand that, Laura,' he said. 'It must have
been very difficult for you, nursing someone you're
close to.'

Once again Laura found herself at a loss, thrown by his perception. And once again, she could find nothing to say.

It was Miss Durham's voice that replied to their knock, and she had brought Sally's morning tea herself.

'I'm glad you're here, Dr Mackay,' she said briskly, 'because I think this little fellow can come out of the incubator and see if he knows how to suck.'

Sally smiled at Laura.

'I'm dying to hold him,' she said. 'That little while just after he was born was much too short.'

David was bending over the baby in the incubator, examining him.

'He seems pretty good to me,' he said at last. 'Let's try him.'

He lifted the baby up and brought him across, his big hands strong and confident on the tiny body.

'Here you are, Sally,' he said, and the girl in the bed reached up and took her baby son a little awkwardly, but so tenderly that Laura found there was a tightness in her throat.

'Hello there, Jeremy,' she smiled tenderly, and Laura, looking at her, thought, not for the first time, that if ever any young woman had a moment of real beauty in her life, it was when she held her newly-born child in her arms.

They waited, she and David, until they were satisfied that both Sally and the baby seemed to know what they were doing, and then David left Miss Durham in charge.

'And just as well I have something to do,' the Matron remarked, 'with almost all my patients at your end! I'm only too thankful, though, that both Mrs Turner and

Mr Wood are improving. And, of course, Penny. Does Irene know yet?'

'I'll go and tell her.' Laura promised.

'Dr Mackay,' said Sally, looking up from her baby, 'it probably isn't fair to ask you yet, but Neil is desperate to see me and the baby. Will it be long?'

David, his hand on the doorknob, met her eyes steadily.

'I can't say yet, Sally,' he told her honestly. 'We just can't risk the possibility of this thing spreading further, even with the antidote available, and there are still a couple of days when a fresh case could show up. As soon as I can make a reasonable estimate, I'll tell you.'

Outside the door, he looked down at Laura.

'And that's true, of course,' he said soberly. 'We'll be keeping on with the daily temperature and blood test checks on all possible contacts, and they'll be doing the same in Cape Town. Just in case.' He smiled. 'Now, off you go and have some sleep, it's been a busy time these past few days.'

But the sound of the helicopter woke Laura an hour or two later. She turned over, hoping to get back to sleep again, but it was impossible, and eventually she gave up, got up and dressed, and went to see if there were any letters for her, as an arrangement had been made for letters for the medical team to be sent from the hospital with the supplies.

There was one from Jane, and one from her mother. She read Jane's first, saving the one from her mother. Jane's letter had been written before the American test drug had been tried, and she sounded sad and depressed, her wedding plans receiving little more than a passing mention, a comment that it was only three weeks now, but neither she nor Stewart could really think of their wedding day, with Penny so ill, and Laura so far away.

But by now, Laura told herself, she'll know that things are looking better. Perhaps, she thought, she might be allowed a quick telephone call to Jane.

And to her family. Her mother's letter, although determinedly bright, couldn't conceal how concerned and anxious she was.

'You seem so very far away,' she wrote. 'Farther away than if you'd taken the job in America.'

Of course, I did think about that a year or two ago, Laura remembered, surprised. And then, unbidden, there was the memory of a girl she didn't know, a girl she had only heard about, who had done just that—because of David Mackay, and the way he had treated her. I'd almost forgotten about her, she realised.

And she wondered, then, if Gwen Lund knew.

But what foolishness, she told herself firmly, to waste time thinking of either of them. As if it was any concern of hers whether there was anything or nothing between two people, neither of whom was her kind of person, and both of whom she really had no time for.

All at once inexplicably restless, she decided to go to the small sitting-room and have a cup of coffee, and sit down with a magazine. But even an article on the next possible twist in Dallas failed to hold her interest, and she found herself thinking of how easy and pleasant and—and plain old-fashioned nice, David had been, when they were with Sally and her baby. And that moment of shared closeness when the baby was born.

And then, blotting out these memories and bringing a flood of shamed colour to her face, there was the memory of that moment in the cave when she had been in his arms, when they had clung together, lost to the world.

Until David had drawn back, had held her away from him. And if he hadn't—

And I suppose, thought Laura, humiliated at the memory, he thinks of that every time he looks at me. But even worse was the thought of the cool hostility and scorn in his eyes when she had, in her confused shame, behaved as if what had happened meant nothing to her. 'I've heard of girls like you,' he had said. 'But I've been lucky enough not to meet any. Until now.'

I hate the man! she told herself now, fiercely—and looked up to see him standing in the doorway, Gwen Lund beside him, laughing as she looked up at him.

Laura stood up.

'I was just going,' she said baldly.

'Don't hurry off,' David replied. 'Gwen and I are just here for a quick coffee break.'

Gwen, barely nodding to Laura, moved over to the small hotplate and poured two cups of coffee. And as she handed one to the big dark doctor, Laura couldn't help noticing—as, no doubt, she was meant to notice, she told herself—that Gwen didn't have to check on how David liked his coffee.

The doctor began to speak about the pleasure of having Sally and her baby here, lightening the gravity of the situation for all of them, bringing a reminder that such things as births and normal life were still going on. And the quiet sincerity of his voice, coming on top of the thoughts that had just been in her mind, was too disturbing for Laura. Suddenly she knew that it would have been easier to see him only as she had been so certain he was—high-handed, arrogant, sure of himself.

'Enjoy your coffee break,' she said abruptly, putting down her own cup, only half finished.

But as she walked out of the room and along the corridor, she saw that the dark-haired girl's hand was on David's arm, and she was saying something to him, softly, so that his head was bent down close to hers.

What I need, Laura told herself, is some fresh air and a good brisk walk. But as she walked at a good pace down towards the river, she found it was less easy than she had thought to put out of her mind the thought of the man and the girl she had just left.

There was just time, she thought, to catch Irene in her lunch hour, and tell her all about the promising signs that the American trip had been so worthwhile.

'Yes, I think everyone in Thornton House knows that the new drug seems to be working,' said Irene as Laura sat down beside her. 'But I haven't heard any details, and no one seems to know exactly how Penny is.'

Laura told her what she could, and although it was little enough, yet they agreed that it did seem to mark a turning-point for Penny. Provided this slight improvement continued.

'It doesn't matter how slow it is, as long as it keeps happening,' Irene said, her voice low. 'In fact, I'd always rather see slow and steady progress than something dramatic.'

Her eyes met Laura's.

'Thanks for talking to Pieter, Laura,' she said gratefully 'There, too, I'm not looking for anything dramatic in his attitude changing, but he does admit that he's begun to look at things differently.' Her blue eyes were shadowed, and her voice bleak now. 'The only thing is, he needs time to work it all out, and time is the one thing he might not have too much of, so I hope he does his thinking pretty quickly! But whatever you said, Laura, it did seem to get through to him.'

She looked at her watch.

'I have to get back to let Gwen off.' She smiled, and Laura thought she was glad to change the subject. 'Our Gwen has her lunchtime worked out to coincide with Dr Mackay's, so I'd hate to interfere with that little arrangement, because Gwen doesn't take kindly to things not going the way she wants them to. I have an idea, though, that she isn't getting much in the way of co-operation from the doctor, and she's not accustomed to that.'

But Laura, with the memory of Gwen Lund and David Mackay as she had left them, close together, their voices low and intimate, wasn't so sure about any lack of co-operation from the big doctor.

When she went on duty later, as she walked past the open door of David's office, he called to her.

'Come in, Sister Kent,' he said. 'I wanted to see you—give me a moment to finish off this report for the research team in America, then I'll be with you.'

Laura stood waiting correctly, professionally, as he finished writing and put the papers in an envelope.

'I'll get that off to Dr Newton tomorrow,' he said, with obvious satisfaction. For a moment he closed his eyes, and she could see that he was exhausted. Then, the signs of weariness gone, he stood up.

'Come through here,' he said. 'I want you to see something.'

There was a window close to Penny's bed, and often, in these long hours of nursing her friend, Laura had stood there even when she wasn't on duty, looking at the still figure in the bed. Now David led her to the window, and without saying a word, pointed inside.

Penny was conscious.

She was very white, and there were deep shadows under her eyes, but she was conscious. She was lying back against her pillows, and she looked very frail.

David tapped on the window and drew Laura forward, making sure that Penny could see her. Laura smiled and lifted her hand, and tried to indicate to Penny that she couldn't come in without a mask and protective clothing. Penny managed a small nod, and there was no doubt, Laura thought, her throat tight, that she had smiled.

'Go and get yourself ready, and you can go in and see her properly,' said David. 'I'm sure that will do her all the good in the world. Oh, there's her chart in my office, you can take it back through with you.'

Laura followed him back to his office and stood waiting as he picked up the chart from his desk. Then he turned round, and she couldn't suppress a gasp of shock, for his face was grey.

'I'm sorry, Laura,' he said, with obvious difficulty. 'I feel—a wee bit strange.'

He swayed on his feet, and Laura instinctively took a step towards him. But before she could reach him, he collapsed.

She knelt down beside him, seeing immediately the clamminess of his skin, her fingers already registering his racing pulse.

He was ill—very ill.

Could it be that the virus he was fighting against had attacked him too?

CHAPTER TWELVE

As she knelt on the floor beside David, Laura had to call on all her training, all her professionalism, and think of what had to be done.

From here, she could use the house telephone, and contact Miss Durham. Then they'd have to get David to the isolation ward, and they'd have to do a blood test. But the only person here who could do blood tests was David himself.

Laura went to the desk and phoned the Matron. All she said was that Dr Mackay was ill, and would Miss Durham please come, but there must have been something in her voice that said more than that, for a minute later, when the door opened, there was alarm on the older woman's face even before she saw the still figure lying on the floor where he had collapsed.

'He just passed out,' Laura told her. 'We'll have to get him into isolation, in case this is the virus.'

There was a stretcher in the corridor, and between them they got the unconscious doctor on to it and wheeled it along to the isolation ward. Jill Derry, on duty there, helped Laura to get David into the bed Harry Wood had been in. The businessman was on his feet again, although confined to this end of the hospital.

'Temperature is up, but only slightly,' said Jill briefly. 'Could mean anything—or nothing. Laura, we need to take a blood test. We can take it here, but there's no one who can test it.'

'I know,' Laura replied, thinking about this. 'Either someone has to be flown in, from Durban, probably, or the sample has to be taken there. Miss Durham, if we can get the blood sample to the police at the road-block, is there any way, quicker than driving, to have it taken to Durban?'

The Matron nodded.

'Yes—Allan Sutcliffe, who farms just off the main road, has a small plane. He would take it.' She looked down at the man in the bed, and when she spoke again her voice was low. 'There isn't anything we can do until we know, is there?'

Laura shook her head. In spite of her hostility to this man, it hurt, almost physically, to see him lying there, his face so grey. She told herself that even if he had contracted the virus, now that they had the American drug there was less cause for anxiety. But none of that helped, nothing seemed to remove the dreadful concern that was making it difficult for her to take even the most straightforward decisions.

Afterwards, she told herself that this was because he was a doctor, and the doctor in charge here. Naturally she felt helpless and thrown when he was ill. Naturally.

They took the blood sample, and Miss Durham went off to take it herself to the police. There was a small research team at the big hospital in Durban, and Jill found the telephone number in David's notes, and phoned to tell them the blood sample would be reaching them.

'They'll let us have the results by phone just as soon as possible,' she told Laura. 'But, Laura, what about our patients here? This new drug has to be monitored every inch of the way—we need a doctor for that.'

Laura turned away from the still figure in the bed, knowing that she had to think, knowing that between them she and Jill had to make some decision.

'I'll phone Dr Marsh in Cape Town,' she said, after a moment. 'I think he'll have to send us someone right away.'

She went through to David Mackay's office and did that, waiting with an impatience she could barely suppress while the village operator made the connection for her. And even when she got through, it took some time for the hospital to locate Dr Marsh.

Quickly, and as clearly as she could, she told him what had happened, and what they had done about the blood test.

'We should have the results of that within a few hours,' she told him. 'Meanwhile—'

'Meanwhile,' the doctor at the other end said, after a moment, 'you do nothing. Keep him comfortable, but give him no medication of any kind. If the test is positive, it's the American drug. But let's face that when it comes. Now, about your position there—I'll have to send someone. It's an emergency, so I think we can call on the Army to help with transport, which means we could have someone with you in a couple of hours. Say four, to be safe. Can you and—Sister Derry, is it—hold the fort until then?'

'Yes, we can do that,' Laura replied, and hoped with all her heart that that was true. She put down the phone and sat at David's desk, thinking about this. There were the three virus patients. Any of them could have a relapse. There was Sally, and her baby. Pieter van Heerden—he too could well need medical attention at any time, and urgently. And there was David himself. Most of all, there was David.

She dropped her head in her hands, almost over-come by the total responsibility of the situation. But only for a moment. Then she told herself firmly that they would just have to do the best they could, she and Jill, until Dr Marsh was able to get a relief doctor to them.

Jill was busy finishing the bedbath she had been giving Penny at the start of all this, and Laura, after telling her what the doctor in Cape Town had said, went over to look at David. Was she just imagining it, or did he look less grey?

She put her hand on his forehead. He opened his eyes and looked at her.

'What's going on?' he asked her, and tried to sit up.

'Lie still, Dr Mackay,' Laura told him firmly.

'Only if you tell me what in the world I'm doing lying here in a bed in—' he looked around him—'in the isolation ward!'

There was nothing she could do but tell him.

'You collapsed,' she said, as steadily as she could. 'In your office. When I'd just come in.'

'Jet-lag,' said David, with certainty. 'I was more tired than I'd admit, and then I sat and wrote up these findings. After that, I just remember thinking I didn't feel too well.'

Laura took a deep breath.

'Your temperature is up slightly,' she told him. 'We've taken a blood sample and sent it to Durban.'

Now he did manage to raise himself up on one elbow, before she could stop him.

'You've done *what?*' he asked, unbelieving.

She told him again. And then, because he had to know sooner or later, she told him of her phone call to Dr Marsh, and that a relief doctor would be sent.

He lay back.

'This is all entirely unnecessary,' he said, his dark eyes on her face. 'I will admit that I'm extremely tired, in fact I don't think I've ever felt so tired. But—blood tests! And someone sent all the way from Cape Town. This is ridiculous!'

Laura kept her own eyes steady.

'Not if you've contracted the virus,' she pointed out. And then, before he could say anything else, 'Dr Mackay, if Jill or I had collapsed, or any of the other people who have been in contact with the virus, you would have treated it extremely seriously. I know you would. I hope you're right, and we have made an unnecessary fuss, but I believe we did the right thing.'

He stared back at her angrily for a long time. And then, quite unexpectedly, he smiled.

'My grandmother would say you're a bonnie fechter, Laura,' he told her. 'A good fighter, in case you don't understand. I must admit I'm very tired. Very tired. . .'

He closed his eyes.

Laura sat beside him, completely still, until she saw that he had fallen into a deep sleep. Then she went across the room to Jill.

'We'll just have to work things as well as we can, for the next few hours,' she said, her voice low, although she doubted if they would disturb the sleeping doctor. 'We'll take turns to have ten minutes off if and when possible. All right with you?'

'All right with me,' Jill replied, busy now with Mrs Turner, and Laura felt a rush of gratitude for someone like Jill working with her.

For the rest of the morning she and Jill worked together, giving each other a short break from time to time, when things were quiet.

It was Jill who took the phone call from Durban, and Laura knew, even before she spoke, that it was all right.

'Not the virus,' said Jill, breathless from having hurried along the corridor. 'Test is negative, so whatever it is, it isn't that.' She looked at Laura. 'You can tell him,' she said, smiling. 'You've already had a blast for what we've done, you can take some more!'

Rather to Laura's surprise, David had completely got over his anger.

'You did the right thing,' he admitted, when she told him that the blood sample was negative. 'I have to admit I'd have reacted in the same way if you—if any of you had seemed to be ill. Anyway, now that the panic is over, if you'll give me my clothes, I'll be getting up and back to work.'

Laura had expected this.

'No, you won't,' she told him firmly. 'There's no reason for you to stay in here, but you can go to bed in your own room, and wait until someone arrives from Cape Town and gives you a complete check.'

Now that the virus had been discounted, another thought was there. This could be a warning sign of a heart attack. The greyness—the clammy skin—

'But we'll take you to your room in style, on a stretcher,' she told him, avoiding his eyes.

'I'm not going to have a heart attack, Laura.'

His voice was quiet, firm, but she wasn't prepared to take any chances.

'I'm sorry, Dr Mackay,' she told him, 'but I'm not prepared to take the responsibility, until you see a doctor.'

Unexpectedly, he gave in, and allowed them to wheel him along to his own room and move him gently into his own bed. Half an hour later Laura, glancing in, saw that he was asleep again.

A small Army helicopter landed an hour after that, and Laura, hurrying to the window, saw Jeff Sheldon coming across the lawn. She went out to meet him, her only emotion relief that they had another doctor here.

'Didn't expect to see me back so quickly, did you?' Jeff asked, setting down a small suitcase. 'I'll be lucky if I've even got a toothbrush, I had to get ready so fast! Right, where is he, and how is he?'

'In his room, insisting that he's only tired. And Jeff, the test is negative,' she told him. She hesitated, then mentioned her thoughts of a possible threatened heart attack.

'I brought a portable ECG machine,' he told her. 'Dr Marsh had the same thought. There it is being unloaded now—I'll go right along and see him.'

Laura went back to work, glad to keep herself occupied, telling herself that now that they had medical back-up she would obviously feel less worried about David. But when Jeff appeared at the door she hurried over to him, her eyes searching his face.

'He's all right,' he said, and there was something questioning in his eyes that made unaccountable colour rise in her cheeks. 'He really is just plain exhausted. I gather that when he went to New York, he didn't sleep on the plane, he didn't sleep at all while he was there, or coming back, and then he threw himself right into a very heavy work-load. I told him he's mighty lucky he isn't about to have a heart attack—anyone's heart would object to that!'

He went over to the other side of the room to collect his protective clothing and his helmet.

'I'll check your folks here,' he told Laura 'By tomorrow, Dr Marsh says we can cut out the barrier nursing.'

She stood beside him as he put on his boots.

'And Dr Mackay?' she asked him carefully. 'What are you doing for him?'

'Nothing,' Jeff told her. 'I've told him to sleep for a night and a day or longer, if he needs it, then I'll have another look at him. Fortunately he seems to have enough confidence in me to feel that I can keep an eye on things here. Penny still improving? The New York trip was tough on Mackay, but there are people who just wouldn't have made it if he hadn't got that antidote.'

There was no cause for concern in any of their virus patients. They had felt that, she and Jill, but it was a relief to have it confirmed by Jeff. A relief, Laura had to admit, just to have him there. For in spite of any personal problems there might be for her—and she hadn't even allowed herself to dwell on that yet—he knew what he was doing, and his casual manner hid an ability and a conscientiousness that she hadn't really realised he had, before seeing him at work here.

But she was glad, too, that he was kept so busy that there was no time for anything personal, glad that her own off-duty times seemed to be when he was at his busiest.

She and Jill, whoever was on duty at the time, checked regularly on David, but doing nothing more than standing at the door and looking in to see if he was asleep. He did, in fact, sleep almost without a break right on into the next day. Laura, turning away from his room and shutting the door gently early the next morning, found Gwen Lund beside her, carrying some magazines.

'I'll just slip in with these,' the dark-haired nurse said easily.

'Dr Mackay is still asleep, and Dr Sheldon says he isn't to be disturbed,' Laura told her, truthfully on both counts.

The other girl looked at her, and her eyes narrowed.

'I won't disturb him any more than you would,' she said. 'I'll just put these magazines down beside him, and leave a note.'

She moved towards the door, but Laura got there first.

'I'm sorry, but Dr Sheldon's orders are very firm,' she said quietly. 'You can ask him, if you like, but I can't agree to your going in without his permission.'

For a moment she thought Gwen was going to push past her, then the girl shrugged and walked off down the corridor. Laura stayed where she was, just in case Gwen came back, and then, just as she was about to leave, she heard David's voice.

'Sister? Sister Kent? Or is it Sister Derry?'

With some reluctance, Laura went back in. He was awake, and sitting up, and although he was unshaven, and his hair rumpled, the grey exhaustion had left his face.

'I'm sorry if I woke you,' she said, a little stiffly, realising that he was aware of her scrutiny.

'Thanks for guarding the door, I don't think I feel quite strong enough for a visit from Gwen,' he admitted.

He ran his hand over his chin.

'I'll feel better when I get rid of this lot,' he said. He looked at the bedside clock. 'Tell Dr Sheldon I'll be along in an hour, once I've eaten and showered. I'm ravenous!'

Laura shook her head.

'I'm afraid not, Dr Mackay,' she told him firmly. 'I'll tell Dr Sheldon you're awake, and he'll come and see you first, and decide whether or not you can get up.'

David sat up straight.

'Damn it, Sister, you can see I'm all right!' he snapped forcibly. 'There's far too much for me to do here rather than lying in bed.' He looked around the room. 'Where are the clothes I was wearing when this nonsense started?'

'I don't know, Dr Mackay,' Laura replied, equably and untruthfully, since she herself had put them in his wardrobe.

'It doesn't matter anyway, I'll wear something else,' David said, and as she looked at him sitting up in bed, his dark hair rumpled, the hospital gown looking out of place on him, suddenly and completely unprofessionally, Laura could see in this big man the boy he had once been.

'I think you should let Dr Sheldon decide, Dr Mackay,' she told him. 'He is in charge of your case, after all.'

'I am not a "case", Sister Kent,' David returned, but she could see, with relief, that he wasn't going to argue with her. 'I'm a busy doctor who's behaved maybe a wee bit foolishly, but that's all. Anyway, you can send Dr Sheldon along. Maybe I'll have a better chance of winning an argument with him than with you!'

Laura turned to go, but as her hand was on the door handle he said her name softly.

'Laura.'

She didn't turn round. 'Yes?' she replied, her voice low.

'Thank you for looking after me so well, and for— keeping me in order.' There was that warmth in his voice—dark brown, straight from the heather, someone had once said, and Laura, against her will, found herself remembering the words.

'All in the line of duty,' she said quickly, lightly—still not looking at him.

'I know that,' he agreed. 'But I wanted to thank you, anyway. And—' she could hear, now, that there was a smile in his voice, 'I won't push my luck by asking if we can be friends, but what about a truce?' He waited, and then said, softly, 'Laura?'

Unwillingly, she turned round.

He was sitting up in bed, and he was holding out his hand to her. And now there was no arrogance, no confidence, no highhandedness. Only a tentative uncertainty, as he looked at her, as he waited to see what she would do.

CHAPTER THIRTEEN

IN that moment, as David held out his hand to her, the hostility between them seemed all at once absurd.

So many things had contributed to it, and had gone on feeding it. His attitude on their first meeting, the things she had heard about him—her own dismay at her unexpected reactions to him, that day of the storm, and the two of them alone in the cave. Too much, surely, to forget and set aside?

And yet—and yet—those other moments, too, moments of closeness, as they worked together, as she saw his concern and his ability. And his humanity.

I've been very foolish about this man, Laura thought with sudden clarity. And very stubborn.

David was still waiting, his hand held out. Laura took two steps towards him and put her hand in his. Both his hands closed around hers for a moment, warm and strong.

'Truce?' he asked, as he released her hand.

'Truce,' Laura agreed, and she smiled, a little uncertainly.

'So we'll give each other a chance?' he said.

'We'll do that,' she replied. It was only, she told herself, because the whole situation was a little unusual that she had this strange, slightly breathless feeling. Nothing more than that.

'I'll go and see if Dr Sheldon is free to come and check you over,' she said quickly, relieved to turn and go out of the room, and conscious, as she closed the door, that David's eyes were resting on her, and that he was smiling.

There was no need, Jeff decided, for David to stay in bed any longer, and provided he did nothing foolish, he could get right back to work.

'I even agreed that he could have a game of tennis by tomorrow,' he said to Laura, telling her this. 'It seems a shame that court standing there and no one using it.'

'We've all been much too busy,' she reminded him. 'Anyway, I shouldn't think any of us gave as much as a thought to bringing tennis things with us.'

'We can borrow racquets,' Jeff told her.

'We?' she queried.

'Oh, yes, didn't I mention that? I promised David we'd take Gwen and him on tomorrow afternoon. You are off, aren't you?'

'Yes, I'm off in the afternoon,' Laura replied. 'But I don't think I—'

They were having a quick coffee together, and Jeff put his cup down, leaned across the table, and covered her hand with his.

'Laura, love, the crisis is over, or well on the way to being over,' he reminded her. 'We all need some relief from it. And what could be better than a friendly game of tennis? Fresh air, exercise—blow the cobwebs away. You'll enjoy it.'

I would, Laura thought, with an honesty that shook her, if Gwen Lund wasn't to be David's partner.

But there was too much in that thought that she knew she dared not let herself examine, so she smiled and agreed with Jeff that a game of tennis would be fun.

And it was, she had to admit the following afternoon. Somehow it didn't matter that Gwen was the only one correctly dressed, her slim brown legs flashing under the flared white tennis dress. Laura and both the men wore jeans, and Laura's racquet was a little too heavy for her, but the game was fun, and she could see in both the doctors a draining away of the strain and the tension they had both been under. Especially David. Once, trying to return a high service from Laura, he slammed the ball into the net, and his shout of laughter at this had Jeff and Laura joining in.

'Wimbledon, here I come,' he grinned, shaking his head. 'Maybe I should learn a few appropriate words from McEnroe!'

But the girl partnering him was less than amused.

'I'm the only one taking this game seriously,' she complained. 'I thought we were to be playing tennis, not fooling around. That shot lost us the set, David.'

'I know it did,' the big Scottish doctor agreed. Over the net, he held out his hand, first to Jeff, then to Laura. 'But you can't always win, Gwen—and you must admit it was fun.'

Gwen smiled, after a moment.

'Sure,' she agreed lightly. 'Sure it was fun. But I find it even more fun when I win.'

For a moment her eyes met Laura's. Or did they? Laura wondered. Maybe I just imagined it.

And even if I didn't, she reminded herself quickly, even if Gwen is talking about much more than a game of tennis, when she says she likes to win—it's still nothing to me. This is nothing more than a very cautious truce between David and me. It doesn't give me the right even to be interested in how things are between him and this girl.

But as they sat under the huge plane tree, drinking tea, she found that in spite of herself she was conscious of Gwen each time she said something to the big dark doctor, each time her slim brown arm brushed against his, each time a word or a look seemed, somehow, to shut the two of them inside a small and private world.

All at once she had had enough. Finishing her tea, she set her cup down.

'Have some more tea, Laura,' Gwen said easily. 'We're going to aren't we, David?'

'No, thanks,' Laura replied, knowing she sounded abrupt and not really caring. 'I have a few things I want to do before I go back on duty. Thanks for the game, folks.'

Walking across the lawn with long, swift strides, she had almost reached the veranda when Jeff caught up with her.

'Hey, remember me—your old buddy?' he said. He was smiling, but there was concern in his eyes. 'What's biting you, Laura?'

'Was it that obvious?' Laura returned, and she smiled too, with difficulty. 'Sorry, Jeff, I'm afraid Gwen Lund is just not one of my favourite people. She gets on my nerves so much that I can't take any more of her.'

'She's all right,' said Jeff, obviously surprised. 'Seems a bright girl—good company, and a good nurse too, I believe.'

'Oh, I'm sure she's all that,' Laura agreed, and she tried to keep her voice light. 'Maybe I'm not feeling too sociable right now.'

Easily, he took her hand in his, swinging it as they went inside.

'I couldn't care less how sociable you feel towards Gwen,' he told her, looking down at her. 'Just as long as you're not feeling anti-social to me.'

'Now why should I be?' Laura said quickly. Too quickly, she knew, because Jeff's eyes were questioning. 'Jeff, I really must go, I have things to do, and I'm on duty again at seven.'

'What things?' he countered, not releasing her hand as she tried to draw it back.

'Washing—letters,' Laura told him, truthfully. But knowing, too, that these things could have waited if she had wanted them to.

'You wouldn't be trying to avoid me, would you?' he asked her, and in spite of the warm teasing in his voice, she knew he was serious. He put his hand under her chin, forcing her to meet his eyes. Any minute, she thought, David and Gwen might come inside, and the last thing she wanted was to be found here, with Jeff so close to her, looking as if—

She drew her hand away.

'Of course not,' she told him. And herself? The thought crossed her mind fleetingly, and she dismissed it. 'See you later, Jeff.'

And in the short time before she went on duty she kept herself very busy, even beginning to pack, for there was no doubt that the crisis was indeed over, that soon the need for their hospital in the hills would be over.

They had now been able to stop the using of protective clothing, and that night, when Laura was on duty, there was an order from David that even normal barrier nursing wasn't necessary now. Daily temperature and blood tests were still being done, but the medical team knew there was now very little possibility of anyone else contracting the virus.

'Tomorrow,' David told Laura and Jill, 'we'll discharge Mr Wood, and we can also let Sally and her baby go home. Mrs Turner has no one at home, and she should take things easy for a bit, so Miss Durham is to keep her here for a couple of weeks. I'm transferring Penny back to St Luke's with us. She's coming on nicely, but she'll have to be in hospital for a bit. Mr Wood and Mrs Turner will both have to have regular check-ups, of course, we can't risk this thing lying dormant and then flaring up.'

He looked up as Jeff Sheldon appeared at the door.

'Ah, Dr Sheldon. I've been putting Sister Kent and Sister Derry in the picture. How about you—do you want to get back right away, or are you prepared to stay? Dr Marsh says it's up to you, they're able to cope at St Luke's now.'

'Then I'll stay, and go back with the rest of the team,' Jeff said cheerfully. 'I'm still not entirely happy about you, I reckon given half a chance you'd be overdoing things again.'

'No, I won't do that. I'm prepared to admit I was a wee bit foolish, and I've learned my lesson,' David replied, embarrassed. 'But—as you wish, Dr Sheldon.'

For a moment his eyes rested on Laura, and she knew he thought that it was really because of her that Jeff wanted to stay. Which, she had to admit, it probably was. And that knowledge didn't make her feel any happier.

'Was there anything else, Dr Mackay?' she asked, hoping he hadn't noticed the warm colour in her cheeks.

'Not at the moment, Sister, thanks,' David replied, and now she could see he was amused at her confusion. 'Dr Sheldon, have a look at this chart, will you?'

Laura left the two doctors and went out into the corridor. As she turned to go and check on her patients, she saw Gwen Lund coming along. The girl was in uniform, but she had unpinned her long dark hair, and it swung to her shoulders. Perhaps you can get away with that here, my girl, Laura thought, but you certainly wouldn't at St Luke's!

'I hope you haven't left David in a bad mood, Laura,' Gwen said, smiling, 'when I'm here to ask a favour. I'm due some leave, and I'm hoping I can get a lift with the rest of you to Cape Town.'

Laura forced herself to ignore the question of why she should have left David in a bad mood.

'I'm sure Dr Mackay will help you if he can,' she returned politely. 'I'll leave you to it, and wish you luck.'

And she walked briskly down the corridor, ignoring the sound of David Mackay's voice welcoming Gwen.

As always when she went back into the isolation ward, her eyes went immediately to Penny. But now she could see an improvement in her friend's condition every time she went on duty. Now Penny was propped up on pillows, and looking around her with interest.

'Thanks, Jill,' she said to the other Sister as she settled herself back on the newly-arranged back-rest. 'Laura, come and tell me everything that's been happening.'

'I can't tell you everything,' Laura protested. 'I haven't time! What do you want to know about, anyway?'

'I want to know what's happening at St Luke's,' Penny said promptly. 'I went on holiday just after the press conference to say they couldn't identify the virus, but it was definitely a haemorrhagic fever. I came right here, and I did hear an occasional radio report, and someone had a newspaper, so I do know that the woman from Saldanha Bay died, but that's all I know.'

Soberly, Laura told her about the other deaths, and about the battle just to hold their own with the virus, until David went to America and persuaded the research team under Dr Newton to release their antidote to him.

When she had finished, Penny was silent for a long time.

'I knew I was pretty ill,' she said at last. 'I was aware of the ventilator, and the tracheotomy tube, and I knew you were there, and Dr Mackay, and then Jeff. But I felt so awful that I couldn't even try to let you know how awful I felt! Does that make sense?'

'Some,' Laura replied, not quite steadily, as she couldn't help remembering some of the dark hours of the night, when she had looked at Penny lying there so ill, and had doubted if they would ever talk like this again. Penny was frail, and there were deep shadows under her eyes, but she was alive, and she was improving all the time. 'I'm just glad we did get the American drug—for you and for the others.'

'He's a honey, Dr Mackay,' smiled Penny. 'Don't you think so?'

Laura bent to pick up the chart she had dropped.

'He's certainly a very good doctor,' she replied carefully. 'They all are, the doctors who've been working on this. I haven't met Dr Marsh, who took over at St Luke's when Dr Mackay came here, but I've talked to him on the phone. And don't you think Jeff is doing very well?'

But she was sorry she had mentioned Jeff, for Penny's eyes lit up.

'Yes, now that was smart of our Jeff to get himself here. How are things with you two? I though perhaps the preparation for Jane's wedding might have spurred you on.'

Laura straightened.

'I really do have a lot to do, Penny,' she said quickly and truthfully. 'You should be resting, anyway. You might have a visit from Irene soon, she was hoping to be allowed in.'

A little while later, when Laura was going off duty, she met Irene coming in.

'Dr Mackay said I could sit with Penny for a little while,' she told Laura. 'I've promised I won't tire her out, but I have something to tell her that I'm pretty sure will make her feel better.' The warm glow in her blue eyes, and the lift of her red—gold curls, told Laura, even before Irene said anything further. 'I don't know what you said to Pieter, Laura,' she went on, not quite steadily, 'but he—he wants us to be married, just as soon as we can.'

Now the blue eyes were clouded.

'It—might not be for very long, we know that,' Irene said, as if she was reminding herself, Laura thought. 'But at least we'll be together for whatever time we do have.'

When they parted, Laura, on impulse, went along to the other wing, hoping to see Pieter, but he had gone out, so instead she looked in on Sally and her baby.

'You know Neil is coming for us tomorrow, to take us home?' said Sally, her baby held expertly over her shoulder as she winded him. 'I can't wait to see his face when he sees Jeremy, when he holds him. Laura, every time I touch him I just can't believe it's true, that he's really here, and he's a strong and a healthy baby. I— I think I couldn't really dare to let myself believe it, after the other disappointments. And then, when things started, and there was no question of getting me to a hospital, I was so worried. But you and Dr Mackay were super—maybe you should be around when we have our next one, you were such a good team!'

Avoiding that one, Laura took the baby from her and held him, marvelling at the way he had progressed in a few days, with the newborn helplessness already lost. His tiny hand curled around her finger, with the strength that always surprised her in tiny babies.

'Is he like your husband?' she asked Sally.

'I think he is,' the young mother replied. 'You can tell me what you think when you see Neil tomorrow.'

The next morning, when Laura was sitting writing up the charts, she saw Sally through the glass panel, beckoning to her.

'I couldn't go without saying goodbye,' Sally said breathlessly, and turned to the tall young man beside her. 'Neil, this is Laura. If it hadn't been for Dr Mackay and her, you wouldn't be holding your son now.'

Laura set the charts down on the desk and went out to say goodbye properly, taking baby Jeremy in her arms for a last cuddle.

'I think you're right, Sally,' she decided. 'Jeremy is like his father.'

'I've left our address in your room,' Sally told her. 'Please do come and see us any time you're in Durban. Oh, Dr Mackay, I'm just telling Laura to come and see us some time, I'd love both of you to see how Jeremy grows. And you two were such a good team, I could do with having you around next time. How about making a date for a couple of years' time?'

For a moment, Laura felt David's eyes holding hers, grave, considering, then he looked away, and told Sally he was sure she would manage very nicely next time, considering she'd done pretty smartly for a first baby, and babies weren't really in his line, but he had certainly enjoyed delivering young Jeremy.

Laura, listening, had a sudden and disconcerting memory of David's hands so strong and safe on the baby's tiny body, and his voice deep and warm as he talked to the newly-born child.

There was something so disturbing in that thought, that memory, that she was glad of the flurry of good-byes, when Jill Derry appeared as well, so that she could say her own goodbye, and then go back to the ward, and the work she had been doing.

CHAPTER FOURTEEN

THERE was so much to do, in the short time left in the Drakensberg valley.

All the hospital equipment that had come with them had to be packed up, some of it to travel with them, the rest to be brought later. There were lists of equipment and supplies to be checked, and to be set out.

And there were the other goodbyes to be said.

A car came to collect Harry Wood soon after breakfast. Laura happened to be outside as he was loading his suitcase into the boot, and after a moment's hesitation he came over to her.

'I'm off, Sister,' he said brusquely. 'I don't know if it's of any interest to you, but I did get things sorted out, and I reckon I won't be sailing so close to the wind again.' He held out his hand. 'No hard feelings?'

'No hard feelings,' Laura replied, shaking his hand. 'You will remember those check-ups, Mr Wood?'

Mrs Turner, too, would have to have regular check-ups for some time. Laura, saying goodbye to her, saw that now that the danger from the virus was over the old lady was rather enjoying the situation.

'Of course I'll have the check-ups, dear,' she assured Laura. 'If that nice Dr Mackay says I should, then that's good enough for me. Now you will come and see me if you're ever in Pietermaritzburg?'

A little later, Pieter van Heerden and Irene came to say goodbye.

154

'We've been to see Penny,' Irene told her. 'I'm sorry she's going now, but at the same time I'm happier to think of her at St. Luke's. She's so much better, but she does still have some way to go.'

Laura set down the list she had been checking.

'Are you two coming to Cape Town for Jane's wedding?' she asked.

For a moment their eyes met.

'That depends,' Pieter told her. And then, his voice steady, he went on, 'If everything is still fine with me, I think we may come. After all, Cape Town would be a good place for a honeymoon!'

Laura watched them go off, hand in hand, and thought, her heart aching for them, it isn't going to be easy, however things work out, whatever time they have. But she felt sure, somehow, that their decision was right for them.

Suddenly, it seemed, the time was gone, and the helicopter arrived, and the lawn of the small nursing home became a hive of activity as supplies and equipment and their own luggage was loaded on. This was a big helicopter, and as they rose above the valley they had a superb view of the Moloti Pass, and the house at the foot of the mountains, the river, and the path, Laura was sure, that led to the cave she and David had sheltered in through the storm.

She turned away, then, not wanting to see or to remember, and found his eyes resting on her. Was he remembering too, or had he managed to forget that time in the cave, before they had shaken hands and decided to give each other a chance?

At Durban they were transferred to an Army plane and taken to Cape Town, and then to the hospital. Everything was done so smoothly, so quickly, that it was only as they drew away from the airport that Laura saw Gwen Lund getting into the airport bus. As they reached the hospital, she wondered if the others had the same feeling of unreality that she had. This morning they had been in the hills, working, involved. Now they were here, back at St. Luke's, and so much had happened while they were away, so much that they had been distant from in every way, that even the long hospital corridors, once so familiar, seemed strange, she thought.

There was a brief meeting when they reached the hospital, with David thanking them for what they had done in the emergency situation.

'You've been a grand team,' he said, looking around. 'We've all been under considerable pressure, and we've all worked very hard. I'm to give you instructions that you all have three days off, and no one is to be back at the hospital before Saturday. That's all, folks. Goodbye—and thanks.'

He turned, then, to Dr Marsh, waiting to speak to him.

And that's that, Laura told herself as she walked out of the hospital with her suitcase. He'll go back to his research in Johannesburg, and I'll go on here. Not that she would have expected anything else, she told herself quickly, for after all, their—truce, he had called it—had come at a very late stage.

We were enemies longer than we were friends, she thought, trying to treat the whole thing lightly. She was glad, very glad, that they had ended up with the hostility gone, and that, surely, was enough.

But he might have said goodbye.

And yet why should he?

She had phoned from the hospital to tell her mother she was coming home, and they met at the station nearest their home. Laura, coming up from the subway, saw her mother standing beside the car, waiting.

'Mum,' she called, and her mother turned round. For a moment, her eyes searched Laura's face, before she held her close.

'You're too thin,' she said, not quite steadily. 'You look as if you could do with a few square meals.'

Laura, knowing and loving her mother, hugged the slim shoulders.

'They haven't exactly starved me,' she replied. 'But I'll certainly enjoy a few days of home cooking. Now, tell me how everyone is, Mum.'

Her mother, easing the small car out of the parking area and on to the main road, glanced at her, just once.

'Well,' she said equably, and Laura knew there would be no probing to hear her own news, until she was ready. 'you haven't really been away so long, although it does feel like ages. Dad's fine—busy, of course, but he likes it that way. Tim's got a new girl-friend—quiet little thing, quite different from that Helen. I like her. Johnny has started taking Sam to training classes, he said he had more time than you do.'

'How does Sam like that?' asked Laura, leaning back and enjoying the familiarity of the tree-lined road close to home.

Her mother smiled.

'He likes the social aspect,' she said, 'but he's not too keen on the homework!'

There wasn't much sign that big black Sam had learned much at all, Laura thought a little later, as his exuberant welcome almost knocked her over. But that was part of coming home, and she found herself wandering around the house and the garden, looking up at Table Mountain rising sheer up to the clear sky, as if she really had been away for a very long time.

'What can I do?' she asked her mother, when they had had a cup of tea, and Laura had rinsed their cups.

'Not a thing, at the moment,' her mother said firmly. 'It's a lovely day, you can almost feel spring around the corner, although it's early. Go and sit in the garden, or have a walk in the wood, and later—'

The phone rang then, and Laura answered it, expecting it to be one of her mother's friends.

But it was Jeff, calling from his flat near the hospital.

'Hi,' he said cheerfully. 'I thought you should be home by now. I tried to catch you to say I'd give you a lift, but you'd gone. I've got these three days off too, Laura—I thought I'd come over and see you. Maybe we could go out somewhere. Cheese lunch at Stellenbosch?'

'Oh no, Jeff, not today,' Laura replied, hoping she had been able to keep the dismay from her voice. 'No, I'm really exhausted, I'm not fit company for anyone. I just want to sit quietly, and close my eyes in this lovely winter sunshine.'

There was a short silence.

'Of course,' said Jeff, with an effort he was unable to hide. 'Sure, Laura—I should have realised you'd be tired. Look, give me a ring tomorrow or the next day, maybe. And have a good rest.'

When they had said goodbye, Laura put the receiver down. And it was a moment or two before she turned and went back to the kitchen.

'Jeff?' her mother asked. And then, giving up the pretence that she hadn't heard, 'You're quite right, love, just give yourself time to unwind.'

And unwind Laura did, sitting in a garden chair with a magazine open, sometimes looking up at the rugged outline of the mountain, but mostly content to feel the sun on her face as she closed her eyes. From time to time there were excited barks from Sam, as he informed her that there were squirrels in the wood at the back of the garden, and so, when he barked even more loudly, Laura didn't even open her eyes.

'You wouldn't catch them, even if I did let you into the wood,' she said drowsily.

'Laura,' her mother called, 'you have a visitor.'

Laura opened her eyes, wondering who had known she was home, and hoping she could hide her resentment at having her peace disturbed.

David Mackay stood on the veranda beside her mother.

'Oh, I didn't—how did you know where I was?' she asked, unable to hide her confusion.

'I asked,' he told her simply. 'I hope you don't mind me coming, Laura.'

'No—no, of course not.'

He looked different, standing here in her own home. Bigger, more casual, and younger.

'I'll make some coffee,' her mother murmured, and disappeared.

Just then Sam came bounding round the corner, tail wagging at full speed, and his teeth showing in what Laura knew was a smile of welcome.

'Good heavens!' David exclaimed involuntarily. 'What kind of dog is he?'

Sam sat down and held out one large black paw. The big doctor, to Laura's delight, just as solemnly took the paw and shook it. Sam, the amenities observed, lay down, his head on his paws.

'His mother was a Labrador,' Laura began.

David smiled.

'But his father was a travellin' man?' he asked. 'Great Dane, perhaps?'

'Probably,' she agreed. 'There was one near enough to qualify.'

'We always had Labradors at home,' said David, rubbing the right spot behind Sam's ears.

'So did we,' Laura returned. 'Until Sam. And actually, until he was three months old we thought we still had a Labrador!'

David told her, then, about the dogs he had had when he was a boy, and the old one still at home with his parents. Laura, refilling their mugs from the pot of coffee her mother had brought out, realised again that just as she had thought she knew this man, she found some other dimension. To see him sitting here, in the garden she had played in as a child, with the old swing still on the tree—it was strange, and somehow disturbing. And yet she knew that she liked the feeling.

'You must be very close to Kirstenbosch here,' David remarked, mentioning the famous botanical gardens.

Laura pointed to the gate in the fence at the back of the garden, and told him that if they walked through the wood, they would be almost at the gates of Kirstenbosch.

'Could we do that?' he asked. And then, hesitantly, 'That's if you'd like to, Laura—if you have no other plans.'

'I would like that very much,' she said softly, meaning it. 'I always like walking in Kirstenbosch.'

They went into the house to tell her mother.

'Good idea, and you could have lunch there if you want,' she suggested, not meeting Laura's eyes. 'Put on your walking shoes, Laura, these sandals will fall to pieces.'

Laura caught David's eye, and saw he was having difficulty hiding a smile. Later, as they walked, he told her that his mother was just the same.

'I don't mind, though,' he said, smiling down at her. 'I think I'd wonder what I'd done wong, if she were to stop fussing!'

'Do you miss your folks—your family, David?' Laura asked him.

'Yes, I do,' he replied. 'I miss them, and I miss Scotland, but I like it here.' He looked up at the bulk of Table Mountain. 'I must say, though, I like Cape Town even better than Johannesburg. There's a feeling of history about things here.'

Laura hesitated and then, carefully, she asked him if he would be going back to Johannesburg soon.

He shook his head.

'Not for a bit—Dr Marsh would like me here to consolidate some of the research.' He glanced down at her. 'In fact, I'm hoping I can keep some of my team from the hospital in the hills together at St. Luke's for a bit. Any objections to that, Laura?'

'None at all,' Laura replied steadily. So there had been no need to say goodbye, after all.

And then, taken aback by the strength of her own feelings, she told him quickly that if he was looking for history, she would take him to see the hedge of wild almonds planted by van Riebeeck right at the start of the settlement of the Cape.

'And what about Lady Anne Barnard?' he asked her. 'She always interests me, with her Scottish connections.'

'If you really feel energetic,' said Laura, 'we could walk up into the forest and see the ruins of her cottage. But it's quite a way.'

He looked down at her.

'Perhaps some other time,' he said softly. As if, Laura thought wonderingly, there were so many other times ahead, for the two of them.

They walked through the lower slopes of the beautiful gardens and admired the velvet sweep of lawn, the old camphor trees, the lilies on the water, and the massed flower beds. Then they had lunch, sitting outside, and grateful for the shade of the bright umbrella even though it was still officially winter.

'My family find it hard to believe it when I tell them about a winter day like this,' said David, taking the cup of coffee Laura had just poured for him.

'We're lucky,' she told him. 'Here in Newlands, close to the mountain, we can have days and days of rain, just as bad as you'd have in Scotland.'

'But not today,' he said, his eyes resting on her face.

'Not today,' she agreed, not quite steadily, for there was something in his eyes that she found extremely disturbing. 'Let's walk to that wild almond hedge.'

When they had found the hedge, and David had admired it, they turned to look at the gardens spread out below them.

'Lovely,' the big doctor said softly.

But Laura, turning to reply, found that he wasn't looking at the bright colours of the gardens.

He took both her hands in his and drew her, unresisting, towards him. They were alone here, for few visitors came up here. He kissed her then, gently at first, and then less gently. When they drew apart at last, he looked down at her, saying nothing. But he took her hand in his and held it as they walked down the path and through the small wood at the back of Laura's home. Her mother was out, and she was glad of that, for she was certain that something of what she felt must show in her face.

'I'll see you back at work,' said David, as he left.

It was only when Laura got back to the hospital, ready for work, that she remembered that she hadn't rung Jeff. It was something of a relief to find that he and David were at a meeting, and wouldn't be around until later. When she did see Jeff, she said to him immediately that she was sorry she hadn't phoned him.

'I should have done all sort of things that I didn't,' she said lightly, but her eyes on his face. 'I haven't even phoned Jane yet, and the wedding is only couple of weeks away.'

'It's all right,' Jeff assured her. 'Some other time.'

Some other time, she thought as he walked away. And she knew she couldn't put off talking to Jeff, getting things clear with him, for much longer.

The entire staff of Block B was kept very busy, for although the crisis was over, and all the patients well on the way to recovery, there was still a great deal of careful nursing to be done, regular monitoring of treatment and condition. David Mackay himself had to submit a complete report both to the Virology Institute and to the American clinic.

Laura, looking in on Penny just before she went on duty, found her friend sitting up, still looking a little fragile, but clear-eyed.

'My mother says you're to come and stay with her when you come out, until they let you leave Cape Town to go home,' Laura told her.

'She'll say I'm too thin,' Penny replied, smiling.

'That shows she's fond of you,' Laura told her. 'See you later, Penny.'

'I never thought I'd find anything to criticise about St. Luke's,' said Penny, 'but you're all so busy there isn't the same time to be sociable that we had at Thornton House.'

I know that, Laura thought feelingly, for although she saw David often throughout the working day, he was usually hurrying along the corridor, his white coat flying, or he was in his office, writing up reports. And Jill Derry too, she reminded herself, Jill and I, and everyone else, we're busy all the time. It was, of course, a short-term situation—when the last of the patients had been discharged, there would be no further need for Block B. And thanks to David's report, the next time something like this happened, medical staff would know a little more about the treatment.

Two days later, just as she was going off duty, Jeff caught her.

'Braai on Camps Bay beach,' he said quickly. 'I thought it was time old David saw something of the pleasant things about living here, before he goes back to the concrete jungle. Jill Derry and her fiancé are coming too—kind of a Thornton House reunion. Oh, and—'

His bleeper sounded, imperiously.

'Damn,' he said, 'got to rush. Pick you up in an hour—don't worry about meat, I've got some.'

And he was gone.

Perhaps, thought Laura, he isn't taking a chance on me saying no this time. But she hadn't wanted to say no, and she knew, very clearly, that that was because David would be there. It wouldn't be like the two of them in Kirstenbosch, but there might be a few moments just to speak. To see, perhaps, if he meant anything by that kiss. And to see, too, if she wanted him to mean anything.

A kiss is just a kiss, she told herself sensibly, it isn't some sort of declaration. But she thought she would know, when she saw him, if that was true, or if his kiss had been something more. And as she and Jeff walked across the moonlit beach to where the others had already started the fire, she could feel her heart thudding unevenly. There he was, his tall figure outlined against the fire. And—

'Hello, Laura,' Gwen Lund, beside David, said smoothly, sweetly. 'So glad you and Jeff could come.' She slipped her arm through David's. 'This is such fun. I'm having a marvellous holiday!'

I bet you are, Laura thought, and was shaken by the intensity of her own anger. Somehow she managed to reply politely to Gwen, to greet David, Jill and her fiancé, and to get out the rolls and butter and busy herself with them.

'This fire will take ages before we can get the meat on,' said Jeff. 'Some wine, Laura?'

He poured wine for her, and beer for himself. And soon Laura, sipping her wine, told herself that there was no real reason to feel so annoyed. Other than the fact that she really didn't like Gwen Lund, and her possessive airs. But after all, it was only her own imagination that made something out of Gwen saying she was having a marvellous holiday. That might be nothing at all to do with David.

A little later, mellowed by her glass of wine, and the pleasant smell of chops cooking, and feeling a little chilly, she decided to collect her thick jersey from Jeff's car, parked a little distance away.

She was on her way back, her own jersey pulled on, and Jeff's over her arm, when she saw the two figures, round the corner from the fire.

Two figures, and then, in the moonlight, the two figures became one.

Laura stood still, sick at heart.

David Mackay—and in his arms, held so close to him, Gwen Lund.

CHAPTER FIFTEEN

NOT caring whether they had seen her or not, Laura turned and went farther down the beach. By the time she reached the fire and the others, she had regained her composure. Or she thought she had.

'You must have run to the car and back—you're quite breathless,' Jeff commented, as she handed him his jersey. 'Food's ready, folks, come and get it!'

Laura felt strangely detached now, almost numb, as she joined the others at the fire. The only thing she knew, very clearly, foremost in her mind, was that she didn't want to think about that moment when she had seen Gwen Lund in David's arms.

The moon had gone behind a cloud, and in the dim glow of the firelight, she didn't see them come back. But they were there, and even though Laura turned quickly to Jill Derry and began to speak, she was conscious of Gwen Lund's laughter, low and soft, as she murmured something to the big dark doctor beside her.

'Good South African custom, a braaivleis, don't you think, David?' asked Jeff, putting chops and sausage on David's plate.

'It's not entirely unknown in Britain, actually,' David replied, amusement in his voice. 'We call it a barbecue, and it's quite popular.'

'Surely you don't have the weather for eating outside?' queried Jill.

'Well now, that's a matter of opinion,' said David, smiling. 'Anyway, I believe, from what Laura was telling me, that Newlands rain can be pretty impressive. Isn't that so, Laura?'

All at once she could hardly bear to speak to him, hardly bear to have him standing there, at the other side of the fire, smiling at her.

'It is quite bad sometimes,' she agreed brusquely, and turned to Jeff. 'Let's sit down on the rug, Jeff, it's more comfortable than standing.'

There was a general movement to sit down, but she could handle that, the whole group of them together. There was one bad moment, when David said to her, from the other side of the fire,

'I've got some beautiful chop bones here, Laura—could we wrap them up and save them for your Sam?'

And as he said it, she was back in the garden at home, such a short time ago, with this man beside her, talking to the dog, stroking him. She had felt so close to him, then. And now—

Childishly, she wanted to tell him she didn't want the bones for Sam, but it was easier just to put them in a plastic bag and thank him, not meeting his eyes, forcing herself not to react to the bewilderment she could see on his face.

But there was understanding on Gwen Lund's face, when they all moved to the sea-facing hotel to have Irish coffees, and Gwen and Laura met in the cloakroom. There was no one else there, and Laura, on her way out, would have gone on quickly, but the other girl put a hand on her arm.

'I gather you saw David and me, Laura?' she asked. And without waiting for an answer, 'I thought I heard someone, but we were—well, rather too occupied.'

'It really doesn't concern me at all,' said Laura, as coolly and as steadily as she could. 'I was just surprised, that's all.'

Gwen raised her eyebrows.

'Surprised?' she echoed. 'But surely, Laura, you realised what our relationship was at Thornton House? I mean, it wasn't a very big place, and you were on night duty sometimes, and no matter how discreet—'

There was no possibility of misunderstanding her.

'Don't look so shocked,' laughed Gwen, amused. 'David is, after all, a normal red-blooded man. Very normal. And very red-blooded!'

I don't have to listen to this, Laura thought, with clarity. And without another word she turned and went out.

Over the Irish coffees, there was a suggestion of driving up Signal Hill to let David see the lights of Cape Town spread out below, but Laura, managing to catch Jeff's eye, said she'd prefer to go home, since she was on duty at seven the next morning.

Jeff was unusually quiet as he drove her back to the hospital. But when he stopped the car, just round the corner from the Nurses' Home, he turned to her.

'We never have had that talk, you and I, have we?' he asked her. Very gently, his lips touched hers. 'But I think, somehow, I've got my answer.'

Laura could say nothing, her throat all at once tight with unhappiness.

'Funny,' said Jeff, after a moment, 'we've known each other all this time, and it's always been fun, and casual, and light, and nothing was farther from my mind than settling down. I just didn't realise how much you meant to me, Laura. Maybe if I hadn't wasted so much time, things would have been different.'

'Oh, Jeff, you'll always be my dear, dear friend,' Laura told him, meaning it with all her heart. For a moment she thought, and surely that's as good as anything to build on? And then she looked at the man beside her. Dear Jeff! He deserved so much more.

She looked at him in the dim light of the car, trying to find the right words, wanting to be gentle with him, wanting to hurt him as little as possible. But there was no kind way to say that she didn't love him, so she said nothing more.

'All right, Laura,' he said at last. 'I guess that says it all. Remember, though, if you want a shoulder to cry on, I'll be around.'

She looked at him, startled. 'Why did you say that?'

He shrugged. 'David Mackay and Gwen Lund,' he replied evenly.

Laura laughed, but she knew her laughter didn't sound natural.

'A little hurt pride, that's all,' she said. 'Believe me, Jeff, I'm not shedding any tears over a man like that.'

And she didn't. That night she lay awake dry-eyed, and thought of all she knew, all she had heard, and told herself she had been right about him from the start; he was everything she had thought he was. That nurse in Johannesburg, the one he had ditched, was well rid of him. And Gwen Lund was more than welcome to him!

Somewhere in the small hours she fell asleep, only to wake to the strident sound of her alarm clock, telling her she had to be in the duty room before seven.

All the years of training and all her professionalism made that possible, and made it possible, too, for her to stand beside David Mackay and Dr Marsh when it was time for the doctors' rounds, to tell them what they asked about, to make a note to follow out all their instructions. Once or twice she found the big Scottish doctor's eyes on her, questioning, but each time she looked away, and throughout that day and the next, it was all right.

But the day after that, when two more patients had been discharged, and the ward was quieter, she was in the duty room, filling in the charts, when he came in unexpectedly.

'Sister Kent,' he said formally, 'I'm glad to have the chance to talk to you. I have the feeling you're avoiding me. Is there something wrong?'

Laura looked up at him, her pen still poised above the chart she had been working on.

'Something wrong, Dr Mackay? No, nothing at all. I'm just rather busy, that's all.'

His lips tightened.

'Very well, Sister, I won't detain you,' he replied.

He's getting the message, Laura told herself, her throat tight with misery. And it won't be long, surely, until he goes back to Johannesburg.

But that afternoon, when she came off duty, he was waiting for her.

'I want to talk to you, Laura,' he said, without preamble.

'I don't think there's anything we need to talk about,' Laura replied, annoyed at the unsteadiness of her voice.

'Oh yes, there is,' he insisted. 'Come into the garden.'

And he took her arm, so that there was nothing she could do but go with him, short of having an undignified struggle.

In the garden, he released her arm.

'What is it, Laura?' he asked her softly. 'Tell me what's wrong, lass. I thought—'

Slow, smouldering anger filled her.

'I don't know what you thought,' she told him shakily. 'But what I think is this: I should have known the kind of man you were, right from the start!'

His eyes were very dark, as he looked down at her.

'And just what kind of man am I?' he asked her.

There was no going back now.

'The kind of man who'll ditch a girl and make her so unhappy she has to go thousands of miles away,' she said, trying to keep her voice steady. 'The kind of man who finds time, even in the middle of a crisis situation, to—to sleep with a girl he's just met.'

She stopped. She had never seen such cold anger in David Mackay's eyes.

'I think that's enough to be going on with,' he said tightly. 'I gather you're talking about Sandra Peters. I don't see why I should give you any explanation, but our parting was mutual. Sandra, in fact, went off to America because of a doctor she had known before she met me, someone she had been very keen on, but her family didn't approve of. You could have got your facts straight, if you'd really got down to checking that out.'

He looked down at her.

'And as for Gwen Lund, I don't know what you're talking about,' he added contemptuously.

'I saw you, on the beach at Camps Bay,' Laura returned, her head high. 'I saw you kissing her.'

'Once again, I don't owe you an explanation, but you saw what you wanted to see. Gwen—seemed to be feeling affectionate. If you'd waited, you would have seen that I managed to persuade her that I didn't feel the same.'

There was something in his voice that told her, to her dismay, that what he was saying was the truth.

'But—but Gwen said—she said that at Thornton House you and she—' she faltered, at a loss.

David was silent for a long time.

'And you believed her,' he said flatly. 'You and I had worked together, we'd known each other—you could have come to me and you could have said David, this is what I've heard, what's your side of the story?'

Laura turned away.

'It was nothing to do with me,' she said, her voice low. 'I didn't mean—'

'I'm not really interested in what you meant,' he told her. 'What really matters to me, just so that we can get it straight, is that you didn't give me a chance, you made up your mind and that was it.'

'I—perhaps I was wrong,' she admitted, with difficulty.

'Oh yes, you were wrong,' he replied, and the cool indifference in his voice chilled her.

He looked at his watch.

'I have a meeting,' he said. 'I don't think there's anything more you and I have to say to each other.'

Long after he had gone, Laura stood there in the small hospital garden. She knew, with complete certainty, that what he had said was the truth. She had misjudged him completely, and worse than that, she hadn't given him a chance. And now she had put an end to the slow, tentative friendship between them.

Friendship?

A tide of colour rose in her cheeks, as she remembered the way he had kissed her, that day at

Kirstenbosch. Gently at first, and then not so gently. He hadn't said anything, but—

Yes, friendship, she told herself. Nothing more, but yet it's sad that I've been so foolish, and put an end to that.

Sometimes, through the next few days, she thought of trying again to say to him that she was sorry, but the hostile remoteness of his dark eyes stopped her. There was nothing she could do now that would cancel out the damage she had already done. It would be better when he went back to the Virology Institute, better when she didn't have to see him every day as he worked long hours to complete his findings for the research team.

Some of the staff of Block B had already been transferred back to the main part of St. Luke's. Laura was more than a little surprised to find that she wasn't one of the team to be sent back. She was glad of that, though, as far as Penny was concerned, for although there was still plenty of work to be done, she could find more time, now, to go in and see Penny, and keep her in touch with their friends.

'I feel as if I've been out of circulation for years,' Penny said wistfully, one day. 'It was nice seeing Jane yesterday, though. I believe the dresses are all ready now.' She patted the bed. 'Sit down and tell me all about everything, Laura. There's only that nice Sister Kent on, and she won't mind.'

In spite of the dull ache around her heart, Laura couldn't help smiling. There was no doubt that Penny was pretty much her old self now.

'Well, just for a few minutes,' she agreed. 'But didn't Jane give you all the wedding news?'

Penny shook her head.

'Jane can think of nothing but their honeymoon in Mauritius, and the problem of whether their bathroom towels should be cream or peach! Well, she did tell me about her own dress, and it sounds lovely, but not much about the other dresses.'

Laura, unable to sit down without a cautious look around, for even if she was the Sister in Charge, it wouldn't do for any of the student nurses to see this informality, closed the door a little.

'Well, my dress is a sort of kingfisher blue, silky material. Very plain style, straight across at the neck, long sleeves, high waist, it follows the line of Jane's dress. You know Jane's little niece Belinda is flower girl? She's the sweetest thing—her dress is the same colour as mine, but with a full skirt, and she'll have a little Victorian posy. I'm told you'll be out in time for the wedding, Penny, so you'll see it all for yourself.'

Penny nodded.

'I told Dr Mackay how important it was, how long we'd all been friends, and he said since I was going to stay with your mother, it was all right, he was sure she'd keep me in order! I didn't know he'd met your mother, Laura—and Sam too, I believe.'

Laura stood up, and straightened the white bedcover.

'Yes, he did come over one day,' she said briefly.

'I believe Jeff is back in the main block now,' Penny went on, and Laura, although glad not to be talking about David, didn't feel too happy talking about Jeff either. 'No engagement coming up at the wedding?'

'Of course not!' said Laura, more sharply than she had intended to, for Penny's eyes opened wide in surprise. 'Sorry, Penny,' she apologised. 'I didn't mean to snap. Jeff and I are good friends, and nothing more—and I really, really mean that.'

Penny looked out of the window.

'Does Jeff know that?' she asked.

'Yes, he does,' Laura told her steadily.

Her friend turned back.

'Well then,' she said, with a lightness that didn't deceive Laura, that made her wonder, now, how she could have been so blind, 'maybe there'll be a chance for a girl who's been eating her heart out for him for quite some time! I'm not in a hurry, I can wait. I can be very patient, if I have to.'

Before Laura could reply, a bell rang out in the corridor.

'I'll have to go,' said Laura, unnecessarily. But at the door, she turned.

'Penny,' she said quietly, 'nothing would make me happier than to see you and Jeff together. I mean that.'

'Me too,' replied Penny, and the steady depth in her eyes belied her jaunty tone.

Laura hurried along the corridor, checking that the bell was ringing in one of the small side wards, where Mrs Masters, one of their last remaining patients, was on her own.

'Hello, Mrs Masters,' she said cheerfully when she went in. 'What can I do for you?'

Mrs Masters, a woman of around fifty, was sitting up in bed. She smiled when Laura went over to her, but her eyes were anxious.

'I don't really know, Sister,' she replied, a little awkwardly. 'I just don't feel quite right. Sort of uncomfortable, and—just not right.'

Laura's heart turned over, but she hid her own anxiety. Surely at this stage there would be no setback in the virus treatment, nothing unexpected? She checked the woman's pulse, and looked at her chart, and although there seemed to be no reason, medically speaking, to justify her anxiety, she had learned, in the years since she qualified, that sometimes you had to go by a feeling.

'I'll have a word with Dr Mackay,' she said, keeping her voice light. 'Meanwhile, why don't you lie down for a bit?' She adjusted the pillows and made Mrs Masters comfortable, before she went out. But on her way to David's office, she stopped at the duty room and got out Mrs Masters' folder. Quickly, professionally, she scanned it, and then her formless anxiety crystallised. This woman had an ulcer. She had been due to come in for examination and possible surgery, when she had been taken ill with the virus.

With the folder in her hand, Laura hurried along to David's office. The door was slightly ajar. He was probably working on the report, she thought, and she pushed the door a little farther, her hand raised to knock.

He wasn't working. He had fallen asleep, his head on his arms. He looked exhausted, she thought professionally. Once again he had gone on doing too much for too long.

And then, as she stood watching the dark head, slowly all her professional feelings left her. She was no longer a nurse, looking with clinical detachment at a very tired doctor, she was a woman looking at a man and longing, with every fibre of her being, to go to him, to cradle that dark head close to her, to stroke his forehead, to put her arms around him and help him to the couch, to put a pillow under his head and to cover him with a blanket.

To care for him.

To love him.

And in that moment, all the pretence was swept away, and she had to admit to herself how she felt about this man. When had she begun to love him? It almost seemed to her that she had loved him all the time, that there could never have been a time when she didn't feel this overwhelming tenderness and caring for him.

David lifted his head, then, and looked at her. Laura could feel warm colour flooding her face, and she was certain that he could read all her thoughts as she looked at him.

His voice was cool and distant, professional and formal.

'Did you want something, Sister Kent?' he asked brusquely.

It took Laura a moment to recover, a moment before her professional training came to her rescue.

Crisply, efficiently, she told him about Mrs Masters, and added that although her pulse and her blood pressure were normal, and there was no clinical sign of any problem, she herself felt, in view of the ulcer history, that they should keep a careful check on her.

David, himself completely professional as well, listened carefully. When she had finished, he stood up.

'Let's have a look at her,' he said, and strode along the corridor, with Laura trying to keep up with him. But there was no sign of urgency about his examination of Mrs Masters, and when he had finished he was pleasant and reassuring.

'Looks as if everything is fine, Mrs Masters,' he told her. 'But there's a chance that this ulcer of yours is playing up again. I'm going to get Dr Anderson—

' he glanced at the folder—'who saw you before, to come over and have a look at you. Meanwhile, rest, and don't worry.' For a moment his eyes met Laura's. 'Sister Kent will look in, and if you want her, just ring.'

Laura, answering his nod, followed him back along the corridor.

'I'd like Dr Anderson to see her right away,' he said briskly. 'As you say, the clinical picture tells us nothing, but you do get a feeling sometimes, and you did well to follow this up. Keep a close watch on her.'

Five minutes later, Laura, coming out of the duty room, met him looking for her.

'Dr Anderson will be over as soon as possible,' he told her. 'Until he gets here, call me if you need me.'

Ten minutes after that Laura, alarmed instantly by a grey clamminess on Mrs Masters' face, found that her patient's pulse was racing.

'Call Dr Mackay,' said Laura to her junior nurse, her voice low. 'And then get back here stat!'

But the younger girl had hardly left the room when Mrs Masters haemorrhaged, swiftly and dramatically. Laura, with the ulcer ever present in her mind, was prepared for this, although she had hoped it wouldn't happen. She got to work immediately, and when David came in a few moments later, he took in the situation right away, and they worked together with barely a word exchanged.

Half an hour later, with a drip set up, and a second pint of blood running smoothly through the transfusion apparatus, the woman in the bed was deathly pale, but the awful grey clamminess had gone.

'She'll do, I think,' David said wearily, standing looking down at her. 'But I'll be relieved to have her taken over to the main block and in Dr Anderson's care.'

They waited, together, until two of the nurses from Dr Anderson's ward came over with a trolley and took Mrs Masters away.

'I'm glad to think of her closer to Theatre, if there should be another emergency,' David admitted, as they stood outside the lift. He looked down at her. 'Thank you, Sister Kent,' he said, and the momentary warmth had gone from his voice. 'You did a good job.'

Suddenly, treacherously, Laura's throat was tight. She knew she could not even try to speak, for tears were too close. Without a word, she turned to go into the duty room. But as she reached it he was there too, his hand covering hers on the door handle.

'Laura—'

She waited, her heart thudding unsteadily, as he looked down at her, his eyes very dark.

He shook his head.

'Nothing,' he said brusquely, and his hand left hers.

And Laura, tears blinding her eyes, went on into the room, unable to look at him, but hearing him walk away from her, so determinedly, so decisively.

It won't be long, she told herself, before he goes, and surely things will be easier then.

With the thought, a wave of desolation engulfed her, for when he went, she wouldn't see him at all, he would be going right out of her life. And yet surely that would be better than seeing him day after day, and hearing him speak to her with that remote indifference that almost broke her heart.

A few days later Penny was able to leave the hospital. Laura had an afternoon off, so she took her friend across to her home close to the mountain.

'I've always loved it over here,' Penny said appreciatively, as Laura parked her car under the old oak tree beside the gate. 'Must be my English forebears—this part of Cape Town always seems very English to me.'

'Right down to the rain!' Laura agreed, as the two girls hurried up the drive and into the doorway.

'I don't mind the rain,' said Penny, and all at once she was serious. 'Maybe this sounds funny, but I don't mind anything. I look around me at all sorts of things and I feel I'm darn lucky to be seeing them, and feeling the rain, and—Hey, your Dr Mackay never warned me that this stupid virus would make me soppy!'

Laura opened the door.

'He isn't my Dr Mackay, and you always did have a soppy streak,' she told her friend. 'What about that bashed old one-eyed teddy bear still sitting in your room?'

'If there's one good quality I have, it's loyalty,' Penny said modestly. And Laura, lifting Penny's case and following her inside, had a sudden, heart-stopping realisation of how different things might have been if David hadn't managed to get the American antidote, if Penny hadn't recovered.

'We're here, Mum!' she called, and her mother answered from the kitchen.

'The door's closed because Sam will knock Penny over, he's recognised her voice. Wait a minute—now you can open the door.'

A moment later Laura opened the kitchen door, and with Penny beside her, went in, to see her small slim mother holding grimly on to the collar of the large and frantic black dog, who was wagging his tail and giving loud barks of welcome.

'He'll calm down in a minute,' Mrs Kent said breathlessly. 'Just shake his paw, Penny, and give him a biscuit.'

Five minutes later the three of them sat at the kitchen table, with Sam lying affectionately on Laura's and Penny's feet.

'And to think I came here for a rest cure!' laughed Penny, shaking her head. 'You must have charmed Dr Mackay, Mrs Kent, he wasn't too happy about me coming out until he knew I was coming here.'

'I certainly liked him,' Laura's mother replied, and Laura wondered if she had imagined her mother's eyes resting on her thoughtfully for a moment. Later, when Penny had been prevailed on to lie down for a little and read the magazines in her room, she found her mother once again studying her.

'I did like David Mackay,' she said quietly. And then, after a moment's hesitation, 'Laura, you know I'm very fond of Jeff, but somehow I've never seen a rightness about the two of you. You may laugh at this, but I did feel that rightness with David Mackay. Was I imagining things?'

Laura turned away.

'No, I don't think you were, Mum,' she said, not quite steadily. 'But I behaved stupidly, and hurt him very badly, and—I guess that's it. But if you don't mind, I'd rather not talk about it, not yet, anyway.'

'Of course not, love,' her mother said quickly. 'I'll just put the kettle on and make some more tea, then I'll see if Penny wants a hot water bottle.'

She bustled around the kitchen, and Laura was grateful for the chance to recover. But she was grate-

ful, too, for the warmth of the quick hug her mother
gave her before she went through to Penny.

It was restful, spending the afternoon at home, sitting at the fire, talking to Penny. And later, putting
on her raincoat and her rubber boots to take the
reluctant Sam for a walk beside the river. As she sheltered under the trees she had the sudden involuntary
thought that David would have enjoyed this.

He had talked, she remembered, of visiting Lady
Anne Barnard's cottage, of walking through the forest to find the ruins. They would have taken a picnic,
and—

Stop it! she told herself firmly, and called to the dog
and turned to go back home.

Her father had just arrived as she got back, and
her brothers, and they had a big, noisy family meal,
with both boys teasing Penny, and Penny, in return,
for she had two brothers herself, and could more than
hold her own, teasing Tim about his new girl-friend.

I'm very lucky, Laura told herself soberly, when
she had said goodbye, and was driving back to the
hospital. I have so much. In time, I'll manage to put
this behind me and get on with my life. And stop
having foolish regrets for what might have been.
Because it was entirely my own fault, and I have to
take the responsibility for that.

Suddenly, it seemed, Jane and Stewart's wedding
was only a few days away. Because she hadn't been
here, she hadn't been able to help Jane as much as
she would have wanted to, but Jane's sister, her fellow bridesmaid, had done a great deal, even to
arranging and holding the kitchen tea just before
Laura returned from the mountains.

She had, of course, seen Jeff at the hospital, but
they hadn't been alone together since the night of the

beach braaivleis, and in some ways she wasn't looking forward to the wedding rehearsal, when Jeff was
best man and she was bridesmaid, and they would
inevitably be thrown together. As for the wedding
itself, when there would be many of their friends who
would think, and say, that she and Jeff might be the
next ones, she couldn't let herself think of it.

But when she arrived at church for the rehearsal,
Jeff came over to her right away, kissed her cheek
lightly, casually, asked about her folks, and Penny,
then turned to the bridegroom to check some detail
with him. Laura's heart lifted, and she was ashamed
of her previous worry. Jeff was an old friend and a
dear friend, and she should have known that he
would do everything to make her feel comfortable.

The rehearsal went without a hitch, and when they
had finished, Jane said her mother had coffee and
cake ready for everyone. Jane's parents lived just
round the corner from the church, so everyone
decided to walk there. Laura found herself with Jeff,
behind everyone else, as he checked final arrangements at the church.

They were almost at Jane's home when Jeff
stopped.

'Laura,' he said quietly, 'maybe I shouldn't ask
this, but how are things with you and David?'

An immediate and instinctive denial of any cou-
pling of her name with his sprang to Laura's lips. And
yet surely to Jeff, of all people, she couldn't be anything other than honest?

She was silent, trying to find the right way to say
what she wanted to.

'As I thought,' said Jeff, after a while. He smiled,
but she could see it was an effort. 'I wasn't too taken

in by that hurt pride business, you know. Why aren't things working out, Laura?'

Laura wasn't sure whether it was because she felt she owed him the truth, or whether she just needed to talk to someone. But she found herself telling him everything—awkwardly at first, and then more easily, until she came to her acceptance of what Gwen Lund had told her about David and herself.

Jeff shook his head.

'She was just out to cause trouble, and you should have seen that, Laura,' he said.

'I know that now,' Laura replied.

She went on, then, to tell him about the things she had said to David, and his reaction. And her realisation that he was telling her the truth.

'But it was too late,' she finished, with sadness. 'He'll never forgive me for not trusting him, for not even giving him a chance, and I don't blame him. So that's it. Come on, the others must be wondering where we are.'

For a moment Jeff looked down at her, and the kindness and concern in his eyes was almost too much for her. She turned and went down the garden path and towards the bright lights.

The next day, the day of the wedding, was bright and clear. Table Mountain stood clear against the sky, and as the bridesmaids stood with the bride outside the small stone church, the afternoon sunshine gave a promise of the spring so close.

Laura adjusted the folds of Jane's veil, and helped the small flower girl to hold the train properly.

'You look beautiful, Jane,' she said to her friend, and it was true. Jane, with her fair hair and her dark eyes, had always been pretty, but today she was so much more.

The Wedding March began, and Jane, on her father's arm, walked down the aisle. Laura, following her, caught a glimpse of Irene's red head, and Pieter beside her. Penny was with them—Penny, still paler and thinner than she had been, but looking better and stronger every day.

The wedding service itself was simple and touching, and over more quickly than she had expected. Suddenly, it seemed, the signing of the register was over and the bridal party was walking down the aisle towards the door, Jane and Stewart together, Laura following with Jeff.

Irene and Pieter, very close together, were smiling at her, and so was Penny. She smiled back.

Then she almost missed a step for there, behind them, looking at her gravely, was David. It seemed an eternity to Laura before she recovered and went on behind the bridal couple. Jeff's hand touched hers briefly, steadying her, and she was grateful for that.

The other bridesmaid, Jane's sister Karen, and the little flower girl, were with them in the car, so neither she nor Jeff could say anything, and the moment they arrived at the hotel for the reception there were photographs, and people arriving, and then they were seated at the tables, listening to the speeches and the telegrams. Laura could never remember, afterwards, if the speeches were long or short, good or bad. David was with Irene and Pieter and Penny, and she found herself determinedly not looking in their direction.

When the speeches were over it was time for the traditional waltz. Stewart and Jane started off, their eyes only for each other, the sheer happiness of their wedding day glowing from them. Then Jeff and Laura, and young Karen and the other groomsman, joined them.

'A little different from our usual dancing, isn't it?' Jeff commented, as they waltzed sedately round the room.

'A little, but nice,' Laura replied.

Then the music became faster, and a number of the other guests rose. Before Laura knew he was going to do it, Jeff expertly guided her to the table where David was sitting.

'Your dance, I think, David,' he said. 'I'm going to keep Penny company.'

There was only a moment when Laura was conscious of Penny and Irene's eyes on her, surprised, but filled with warmth and with love. Then David's arms were around her, and they were dancing, both of them formal, stiff.

'I didn't expect to see you here,' said Laura, as the silence between them seemed to become even heavier.

'Jeff arranged it,' David told her. 'He came to see me last night.'

Laura missed a beat, and their feet became tangled.

'I can't talk to you here, Laura,' said David abruptly. He took her hand and led her off the dance floor, and out to the garden.

He was still holding her hand, and after a moment he took her other hand as well, holding them both between his own.

'Jeff made me see what a fool I was,' he said at last, looking down at their clasped hands. 'Pride is a terrible thing, Laura, and my pride was hurt. I told myself I could never forgive you, for the way you had judged me, for the way you'd believed what you did, without giving me a chance. But that was my pride, and pride is a lonely thing, Laura.'

He released her hands and looked down at her.

'I wouldn't want you to be lonely, David,' she said, not quite steadily.

His eyes held hers, steady, searching, making certain of what she was telling him. And then, without saying anything more, he took her in his arms and kissed her, gently at first, then not at all gently.

It was a long time before they drew apart.

'I think we'd better go back inside, Laura lass,' David murmured, his lips still close to hers.

'I think we had,' Laura agreed. 'This is Jane and Stewart's day.'

And for us, she thought, soberly, thankfully, this is just the beginning. We have time—time to get to know each other, time to let this new love grow properly.

His lips brushed hers briefly, warmly, with a promise of all the time ahead of them.

'Time to go, Sister Kent,' he told her.

'Whatever you say, Dr Mackay,' she replied, demurely, lovingly.

They went back in to the wedding reception, her hand in his.

Incurable romantics read one before bedtime.

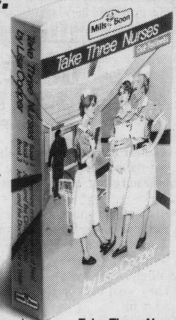

Josephine, Jane and Jacinth were a trio of friends who as students at the Princess Beatrice Hospital in London shared the first years of hard work, laughter and tears.

But now the training is over and the time has come for them to go their separate ways as fully fledged nurses and midwives.

Take Three Nurses is series of three stories t follow the individual fortunes each of the three girls on road to success and romance

Josephine and a Surgeon of Steel

Jane and the Clinical Docte

Jacinth and The Doctor Make a Wish

TAKE 4
DOCTOR NURSE
ROMANCES

AND THRILL TO THE HEARTACHE AND DRAMA OF HOSPITAL LIFE.

THEY ARE YOURS **FREE!**

Reaching the end of a wonderful romantic story is always a little sad – even if it has a happy ending. So why not continue your reading pleasure with four marvellous Doctor Nurse stories – they're yours for the asking, absolutely free. It's our special offer to introduce you to Mills & Boon Reader Service. Thousands of regular romance readers use our subscription service. When you see the benefits you can enjoy as a subscriber we think you'd want to join them. See overleaf for details of our exciting FREE offer…

Mills & Boon

▶▶▶